MARIE-HÉLÈNE LEBEAULT
AUTHOR OF THE EVERS SERIES

A CURSE OF
SNOW
AND
ASH

A SNOW WHITE RETELLING

CHAPTER I

THE HUNT BEGINS

Valira's eyes snapped open, stinging with the frigid air. She could feel the sharp bite of the cold against her skin, but she didn't flinch. The snow beneath her had melted from the heat of her body, leaving a damp spot on her clothes. Glimpses of steel-colored sky peeked through heavy clouds, casting a dreary light on the snowy landscape. With a shiver, she sat up and brushed off frost from her hair, revealing strands as white as the ground beneath her. Something was off about this morning, and Valira couldn't shake the feeling of unease that settled in her gut.

Sinking deeper into the snow, Valira struggled to move her numbed fingers. Despite the frozen world around her, a simmering heat pulsed in her chest. It was the only thing keeping her going.

She stood up and took in her surroundings. Trees

were stripped bare of leaves, their branches coated in a layer of ice. The air smelled of snow, crisp and clean, like freshly washed laundry. How had she ended up here? She couldn't remember anything before a sharp pain and the feeling of falling.

As she walked forward, she noticed something strange: her feet left no footprints in the snow. She blinked and tried to clear the fog in her mind. With each step, her heartbeat remained steady, almost unnaturally so. The silence of the forest seemed to stretch on forever.

Until a sudden sound shattered it - a distant howl that sent shivers down Valira's spine.

A small crack echoed through the stillness of the forest, causing Valira to freeze in her tracks. She immediately became alert, her senses sharpening as she scanned the area for signs of danger. And then she saw him, a figure cloaked in dark fur, standing at the edge of the clearing with an air of silent menace.

His eyes were piercing, cold and calculating as they locked onto hers and his hand rested on the hilt of a long, silver blade. Valira's heart raced, fear gripping at her chest. She didn't know who this stranger was or what he wanted, but she knew he wasn't here to help her.

In trepidation, Valira raised her hand and felt a warmth spreading through her chest, traveling down her arm and into her fingers. The snow at her feet melted in a perfect circle, steam rising from the ground. She was both amazed and terrified by this unfamiliar power coursing through her veins.

The man hesitated for a moment, his grip on his sword loosening as he looked down at the melted snow with surprise. He spoke in a low, measured voice. "You shouldn't be here."

Valira's heart pounded in her ears as she responded defiantly, "Neither should you."

But before either of them could say anything else, a distant rumble grew louder and shook the ground beneath them. Valira turned to see a fireball hurtling towards them from behind the man. In a split-second decision, the force of the fire threw him aside, colliding with a nearby tree and setting it ablaze.

Valira stumbled back in shock as figures emerged from shadows engulfed in flames. Their eyes glowed with an eerie orange light that matched the color of the forest fire surrounding them.

They were not human.

Valira's skin prickled as the heat from the fire engulfed her, but it was more than just the flames that made her uneasy. The eyes of the approaching figures glowed like embers and their movements crackling with an otherworldly energy. She took a step back, her heart pounding in her chest.

As the man struggled to his feet behind her, Valira's eyes darted between him and the fiery figures. She felt a surge of hope that he would protect her, but his next words shattered that illusion. He barked at the creatures, positioning himself between them and Valira, sword at the ready. "Stay back," he commanded. "This one is mine."

The creatures paused, amused by his bravado. The leader - a tall woman with skin like molten lava and hair that burned like fire - hissed out a biting response, "Yours? She belongs to the Ash Court."

Valira's confusion turned to fear as she heard those words. The Ash Court? Her? It didn't make sense, but she had no time to dwell on it as the fiery woman raised her hand and shot a stream of fire directly at the man.

With quick reflexes, he dodged to the side, his cloak singed by the heat. Valira felt a surge of gratitude towards him, but then he turned to her with urgency in his eyes. "Run."

For a moment, Valira hesitated—where could she possibly run to? But there was no time for questions as another blast of fire erupted behind her. With shaking legs, she turned and fled into the forest, the sounds of battle ringing in her ears. Fire clashed with ice as she ran, but she didn't dare look back. All she could think about was surviving this chaotic encounter.

As she sprinted through the dense forest, Valira's calves ached and her lungs burned with each gasping breath. The trees raced by in a green blur, but still she pushed herself faster, desperate to escape. Suddenly, a figure appeared ahead of her, standing tall and unharmed despite the raging fire that surrounded them.

Valira skidded to a stop, her heart pounding against her ribcage. It was him—the man with ice-blue eyes that seemed to see right through her. He took a step closer, his voice calm and unnerving.

"Where do you think you're going?" he said, reaching out to grab her arm with an ice-cold grip. Valira tried to pull away, but his strength was impossible to overcome. Panic rose in her chest as she frantically searched for an escape, but the man's words stopped her.

"You can't outrun them," he whispered. "And you can't outrun me."

Her mind raced as she tried to process his words. Who was this man? And why did his touch feel so strangely familiar?

Before she could find an answer, he spoke again. "I was sent to kill you."

Valira's stomach dropped at his chilling words. She should have been terrified, but she felt a strange sense of inevitability wash over her. Of course, someone had been sent to kill her. It made sense.

"Why haven't you?" she asked in a shaky voice.

The man's stony gaze flickered for a moment before returning to its steady state. "I haven't *yet*," he replied cryptically.

A shiver ran down Valira's spine as she realized the gravity of the situation. But despite her fear, there was something about this man that compelled her to ask one more question.

"Who are you?" she whispered.

For a split second, his eyes softened with a hint of remorse before hardening once more. "I am your assassin."

The man's grip on Valira's arm was firm, his dark eyes flickering with indecision. For a moment, they stood in tense silence as he studied her face, trying to decide whether to trust her. Finally, he let go of her and muttered, "Something's not right. You're not what they said you were."

Before Valira could ask for clarification, a loud roar echoed through the forest behind them. She turned just in time to see a woman wreathed in flames running towards them, setting the trees ablaze in her wake. Panic set in as Valira realized she was being pursued.

Without hesitation, the man grabbed her hand and pulled her towards a denser part of the forest. "Run!" he commanded, his voice brooking no argument.

Valira ran beside him, their feet pounding against the frozen ground as they fled from their pursuer. But it wasn't just fear that drove them forward - there was a sense of urgency building inside Valira, something warm and powerful that threatened to burst forth at any moment.

They reached the edge of a frozen ravine and skidded to a stop. The man quickly assessed their surroundings before turning to Valira with determination in his eyes.

"You can't run forever," the fiery woman yelled. "She belongs to the Ash Court. Hand her over and I'll spare your life."

Valira's heart raced as she tried to make sense of everything. Fire, ice, courts - it all felt like pieces of a puzzle that refused to fit together. But one thing was clear: this woman wanted more than just Valira's capture.

Before Valira could say anything, the man called out, his voice steely. "I don't care which court she belongs to. She's not yours!"

He raised his hand, and suddenly the air shifted. Ice spread from his fingertips, forming a bridge of frozen water over the ravine.

"Now," he said, his voice urgent but determined, "Run."

As they raced across the icy bridge, each step cracking beneath their feet, Valira could feel the frigid air biting at her skin. The man beside her was swift and sure-footed, his dark hair whipping in the wind as he gripped her hand. Behind them, a woman wreathed in flames screamed in anger, her fiery tendrils licking at the edges of the bridge but unable to cross the expanse of ice.

Valira's heart pounded with every step, and she could feel a heat building inside her that was unfamiliar and intense. Just as they reached the other side of the ravine, the ice bridge crumbled beneath their feet with a deafening roar. Without stopping, the man pulled her into the thick cover of trees, his grip unyielding and his pace relentless.

"Where are we going?" Valira gasped, struggling to keep up.

"Anywhere she can't follow," he replied sharply, scanning their surroundings with wary eyes. "We need to find shelter."

Valira's legs burned with exhaustion, but she pushed herself to keep running. The forest seemed to close in on them, the towering trees forming a dense canopy that blocked out the sun. After what felt like hours, the man finally slowed down and led her behind a massive boulder covered in frost.

The cold seeped into Valira's bones, but she could feel something warm and powerful coursing through her veins, keeping her from freezing. The man released her wrist and took a step back, his breath visible in the chilly air. For the first time, she noticed how young he was—no older than she—with sharp features and a strong jawline. He ran a hand through his dark hair, his expression grim and determined.

Valira's heart raced as she collapsed against the rough surface of a boulder. Her companion muttered something under his breath and looked over his shoulder. The sense of danger was palpable in the air.

"Who was that?" Valira asked, her voice trembling. "Why is she after me?"

The man turned to face her, his expression hard and guarded. "That was one of the Ash Court's hunters. They've been searching for you for a long time."

Valira's confusion grew as she tried to make sense of everything. "Me? But why? I don't even know who I am. I don't remember—"

"Exactly," he cut her off, his voice cold and detached. "You don't remember because they made sure of it. They wiped your memories, hid you away, and now they want you back."

A surge of fear and anger rushed through Valira's veins. "Why would anyone do that?"

"Because you have power," the man said, his gaze flickering with an unreadable emotion. "A power that could tip the scales in the ongoing war between our realms."

Valira's mind reeled at this revelation. She didn't understand why she had this power or how it could be so dangerous.

"And what about you?" she asked, her voice shaking slightly. "How do you fit into all this?"

The man's jaw tensed as he crossed his arms over his chest. "I was sent to kill you," he said bluntly.

Valira felt like the ground had dropped out from under her. "Kill me?"

He nodded grimly. "My father, the King of the Snow Court, ordered your death. He sees you as a threat to our kingdom."

Valira couldn't believe what she was hearing. None of this made sense—the Ash Court wanting her, the Snow Court wanting her dead, and this strange power that she couldn't control. She stumbled backward, her heart pounding in her chest.

"Please," she pleaded with the man. "I don't understand any of this. Can you help me?"

The man's expression softened for a moment before hardening again. "I was sent to kill you, but I won't do it. Not without hearing your side of the story first."

Valira's eyes widened at his words. Was there a chance for her to survive after all? To find out who she truly was? She could only hope as the man continued to speak about the dangers that awaited them in the coming days.

Valira's heart was racing as she whispered, "What am I?" to the man standing before her. His eyes softened for a fleeting moment, but then the coldness returned. He replied, "You're the Ash Princess—born of fire and flame, destined to destroy." Her stomach twisted at his words, and she desperately shook her head in denial. She couldn't be a destroyer.

But then he asked if she had felt it - the heat inside her, the fire that burned within. Valira looked down at her trembling hands, remembering the flames that had burst from her when the Ash hunters attacked. It was all too much to comprehend.

"I don't want to destroy anything," she whimpered.

The man sighed, his face softening slightly. "I know. But that doesn't change the fact that you're a danger to both courts."

Desperation crept into Valira's voice as she asked why he hadn't killed her yet. He hesitated before answering, his gaze searching hers. "Because you're not what I expected. You're... different."

Her heart skipped a beat at his words, but she didn't dare believe them fully. "Different how?"

The man looked away, struggling to find the right words. "I can't explain it. But there's something about you... something that doesn't match everything I've been told. And until I figure out what that is, I'm not going to end your life."

Relief flooded through Valira's chest at his words, but it was short-lived. She couldn't ignore the truth - he was here to kill her.

She swallowed hard and mustered up enough

courage to ask for his name. He met her gaze and finally replied, "Caelan. Prince of the Snow Court."

"Caelan," Valira repeated, the name sounding foreign on her tongue. She studied him carefully, trying to reconcile the person standing in front of her with the one who had been sent to end her life. A prince—someone who lived in castles, commanded armies—now standing with her in the wilderness, his mission unclear. Her pulse quickened as the weight of his admission sank in.

"Prince of the Snow Court," she murmured, still trying to grasp the enormity of it. She had only heard fragments about the courts in her hazy memory—legends, mostly. Snow and Ash. Cold and flame. Endless war.

But now, standing face-to-face with the prince, she realized those stories were very real.

"Why do they want me dead?" she asked, her voice barely above a whisper. "I don't understand."

Caelan's jaw tightened, and he turned his gaze toward the forest, scanning the shadows. "You're not just any Ash Princess. You're the product of a forbidden union—fire and ice. The Snow Court believes you're a weapon, one that could destroy both kingdoms."

Valira's heart raced, her mind spinning with the new

information. Her? A weapon? The words made no sense. She had no memory of any union, no recollection of being anything but... lost. But deep down, the warmth simmering beneath her skin, the way her powers had erupted in the heat of danger—it was undeniable.

"They think I'm dangerous," she said, more to herself than to him. "But I don't even know how to use these powers. I didn't ask for them."

Caelan glanced at her, something softening in his gaze. "Maybe that's why I haven't killed you," he admitted quietly. "You don't seem like the weapon they fear."

Valira's breath caught in her throat. "So, what now?"

Before Caelan could answer, a rustling sound came from the trees. Both of them tensed, their eyes snapping to the darkened forest. The silence that followed was thick and unnerving, broken only by the faint crackle of leaves underfoot.

Suddenly, a fiery arrow shot through the air, embedding itself into the tree just inches from Valira's head. She gasped and ducked, her heart leaping into her throat.

"They've found us," Caelan growled, drawing his sword in one fluid motion. His stance shifted, his entire body bristling with readiness as his eyes darted across the shadows.

Valira barely had time to react before another arrow

flew, this one aimed directly at her chest. But before it could strike, Caelan moved too fast for her follow, deflecting the arrow with a sharp flick of his blade. Sparks flew, the air hissing with the clash of fire and steel.

"Run," Caelan commanded, his voice rough with urgency. "I'll hold them off."

Valira froze, her mind racing. Running felt like the only option, but something deep inside her told her she couldn't leave him here—not alone, not against whatever was coming.

But before she could protest, the forest erupted in flames. Figures, cloaked in fire, stepped out from the shadows, their eyes glowing like molten embers. There were more of them now—at least six. All armed, all moving with deadly precision.

Valira's breath hitched as one of them stepped forward, a man with flames licking at his fingertips, his eyes trained on her like a predator watching its prey.

"The Ash Queen sends her regards," he hissed, raising his hand. Fire swirled in his palm, ready to strike.

Valira's pulse pounded in her ears. She could feel the fire inside her responding, like a spark igniting in her chest. It wanted to be unleashed, to match the flames that surrounded them, but she didn't know how to control it. Panic surged through her.

Caelan moved in front of her, his sword raised, his voice a low growl. "You'll have to go through me first."

The man sneered, but before he could attack, Valira felt something shift inside her—something powerful, something terrifying. The heat in her chest swelled, rising like a wave, and before she could stop it, flames erupted from her hands, surging toward the enemy in a fiery arc.

The man screamed as the fire engulfed him, his body consumed in a blaze of orange and red. The other attackers staggered back, shocked by the sudden display of power.

Valira gasped, stumbling as the fire inside her receded, leaving her breathless and shaken. She looked down at her hands, still trembling, her heart racing with fear and disbelief.

"What... what just happened?" she whispered.

Caelan turned to her, his expression unreadable. "You tapped into your power."

"I didn't mean to," she stammered, her voice shaky.

Caelan's eyes softened, but only for a moment. "Doesn't matter. We have to move. Now."

Without another word, he grabbed her hand, pulling her away from the scene of destruction. The forest blurred as they ran, the heat from the battle still lingering in the air.

But in the pit of her stomach, Valira knew the real battle was only just beginning.

Valira's pulse hammered in her ears as she and Caelan wove through the dense, frostbitten trees, their footsteps muted by the snow underfoot. The fire in her chest had dimmed, but its echo lingered—an unsettling reminder of the power she couldn't control. The attackers were behind them, distant for now, but she could still feel the heat from their approach in the air. There was no time to stop, no time to question what had just happened.

Caelan's grip on her hand was tight, guiding her through the labyrinth of ice-bound trees, his breath steady and focused. He didn't speak. He didn't need to. The silence between them was thick with tension, but also something else—an understanding that their survival now depended on each other.

After what felt like miles, they finally reached the edge of the forest, where the trees thinned, giving way to a vast, frozen plain. Caelan slowed, glancing over his shoulder to check if they were still being followed. The sky had darkened, clouds gathering overhead, and the wind cut sharply against Valira's skin.

"We need to rest," Caelan said, his voice low and cautious. "But not here. We'll be too exposed."

Valira nodded, her breath coming in ragged gasps, exhaustion threatening to overtake her. The power she had unleashed earlier had drained her more than she realized. Every muscle in her body ached, and her legs felt like they might give out at any moment.

They moved toward a rocky outcrop, a jagged formation rising out of the snow like a forgotten ruin. It provided some cover from the biting wind, and Caelan motioned for her to sit. She collapsed onto the cold stone, her mind still racing from everything that had happened.

For a long time, they sat in silence; the wind howling. Valira stared at her hands, the memory of the fireball she had conjured flashing through her mind. She didn't know how she had done it, didn't understand what had triggered it. But the fear that had gripped her in that moment... it had felt like she was losing control.

"Are you all right?" Caelan asked, his voice softer than before.

Valira looked up, meeting his gaze. For a prince sent to kill her, there was an odd gentleness in his eyes—an understanding, perhaps, of what it meant to carry a burden like hers.

"I... I don't know," she admitted, her voice barely above a whisper. "That fire... I didn't mean for it to happen. I just..."

Caelan nodded, his expression grim. "That's what makes you dangerous. The Ash Court will use that power, and the Snow Court will fear it. It's why they want you gone."

"But I don't want to hurt anyone," Valira said, her

voice trembling. "I don't even know how to control this."

"You will have to learn," Caelan said, his tone firm. "If you can't, then they'll use you... or kill you."

Valira shuddered at his words. The weight of her situation pressed down on her like an avalanche. She was trapped between forces, both determined to use her or destroy her. And the worst part? She didn't even know who she really was. The memories of her life before the forest were a blank slate, leaving her to piece together the fragments of a history she didn't remember.

Caelan's gaze softened as he watched her struggle with the realization. "Look, I'm not your enemy," he said quietly. "I was sent here on a mission, but everything has changed. Whatever you are, whatever power you have, I think it's more than either of the courts understand."

Valira blinked, surprised by the sincerity in his voice. "Then why help me?"

Caelan hesitated, his eyes flickering with uncertainty. "Because I don't think you're the threat my father believes you are. And... maybe because I don't want to be the one who decides your fate."

Valira's heart thudded painfully in her chest. There was so much she didn't understand—about herself, about the world she had been thrust into, about Caelan. He was a prince, a hunter, someone bound by loyalty to the Snow Court, yet here he was, standing between her and the forces trying to claim her life.

A heavy silence hung between them as the wind howled louder, carrying with it the promise of an approaching storm. Valira wrapped her arms around herself, trying to ward off the chill creeping into her bones. But it wasn't just the cold. It was the fear—the fear of what she might become if she couldn't control the fire within her.

"We can't stay here," Caelan said after a long pause. "The storm will cover our tracks, but it'll freeze us if we don't move."

Valira nodded, struggling to her feet. Every part of her ached, but she knew he was right. They couldn't stop now. Not when the Ash Court was still hunting them.

As they moved through the growing wind, Valira stole a glance at Caelan. He had saved her life—more than once now. And even though she couldn't fully trust him, something inside her told her he was more than just her enemy.

She just hoped she wouldn't regret it.

The storm swept in quickly, snow whipping through the air like icy daggers. But even through the haze, Valira felt a strange pull, something deep inside her stirring, guiding her toward something she couldn't yet see.

And in that moment, she realized her journey was only just beginning.

CHAPTER 2

THE COURT OF ASH

Caelan stood at the cave entrance, the wind howling outside as he peered into the swirling snow. His sword, still sheathed at his side, felt heavier than usual, weighed down by more than the battles they had just fought. The air inside the cave was cold, but it was nothing compared to the frost creeping through his thoughts.

Valira had fallen asleep against the rocky wall, her breath steady, her body still recovering from the burst of power she'd unleashed. Caelan watched her for a long moment, the flicker of flames from her earlier display still fresh in his mind. It wasn't just her power that unsettled him—it was the way she had balanced the fire and ice, a harmony he hadn't thought possible.

His father had been wrong. Valira wasn't just some

weapon to be destroyed. She was more. And that terrified him.

He turned his gaze back to the storm, his thoughts churning. The Snow Court wouldn't stop hunting her. Neither would the Ash Court. And now, caught between both worlds, Caelan was forced to make a choice he hadn't been prepared for.

There was a movement behind him, and he turned to see Valira stirring. She blinked, groggy but alert, her eyes flicking toward him with a mixture of exhaustion and curiosity.

"Didn't think you'd get any sleep," Caelan said quietly, his voice barely audible over the wind.

"I didn't mean to," Valira admitted, sitting up and rubbing her eyes. "But I guess my body had other plans."

Caelan nodded, his gaze still distant. He could sense the question lingering on her lips—the question she had every right to ask. Why was he helping her? Why hadn't he killed her? Caelan wasn't sure of the answer anymore.

"I don't understand you," Valira said suddenly, breaking the silence.

He looked at her, brow furrowed. "What do you mean?"

"You could've finished me back there," she continued, her voice soft but unwavering. "You had orders and plenty of chances. But you haven't."

Caelan didn't respond immediately, his fingers tightening around the hilt of his sword as he considered his answer. The easy response would've been to say that he was biding his time, waiting for the right moment. But it wasn't the truth, and they both knew it.

"I told you," he said after a long pause. "You're not what I expected."

Valira's eyes narrowed, suspicion flickering in her gaze. "And what did you expect?"

Caelan let out a slow breath, his gaze dropping to the floor. "I expected a monster. A force of destruction. But you're not that."

She said nothing, but he could feel the weight of her stare, the silent challenge hanging between them. Valira would not be satisfied with vague reassurances. She needed answers. And so did he.

He stepped away from the cave entrance, kneeling beside her, his expression serious. "You don't know what you're capable of," he said. "The courts fear you because they've never seen anything like you. But that doesn't mean you're the threat they think you are."

Valira met his gaze, her voice soft but filled with determination. "I don't want to be a threat. I don't want to hurt anyone."

"I know," Caelan said. "But until you learn to control what's inside you, the courts won't see it that way."

She bit her lip, her eyes filled with uncertainty. "How do I control it? I barely know what I'm doing."

Caelan's jaw tightened. He didn't have an answer for that, either. He had spent his life mastering the cold, honing the power of ice that flowed through his veins. But Valira... she was something entirely different. A force that couldn't be bound by a single element.

"I don't know," he admitted. "But I'll help you figure it out."

Her eyes widened, surprise flashing across her face. "Why? Why would you help me when you were sent to kill me?"

Caelan hesitated, his mind racing through the reasons he had told himself over and over. Duty. Guilt. Curiosity. But deep down, there was something else—a flicker of something he didn't want to name.

"Because I think you're the key to ending this war," he said, his voice low. "And because... maybe I don't want to follow my orders anymore."

Valira looked at him, a mixture of hope and doubt swirling in her gaze. She was struggling to understand her power, identity, and role in a world that deemed her dangerous. Caelan understood that. Despite controlling her power, enemies would surround her on the road ahead.

The storm outside died down, the howling wind softening into a faint whisper. Caelan stood, his expression hardening once more as he strapped his sword to his side.

"We need to move before they find us again," he said, offering his hand to her. "The Ash Court won't stop until they have you."

Valira took his hand, her grip firm despite the uncertainty in her eyes. She stood beside him, her shoulders squared as if preparing for the weight of what was coming.

"And the Snow Court?" she asked quietly.

Caelan's jaw clenched. "They won't stop either. But I won't let them take you."

Valira nodded, and without another word, they stepped out into the fading storm, the frozen wasteland stretching before them. Valira, for the first time, felt hope despite the long, dangerous journey ahead.

She wasn't alone. Not anymore.

Maybe she could control the warring fire and ice.

The snowstorm had subsided into a faint, icy breeze, leaving a thick blanket of white across the forest floor. Valira and Caelan trudged through the snow in silence, their breath forming misty clouds in the cold air. The storm may have passed, but the weight of their situation hadn't lifted.

Valira's mind was a jumble of thoughts, her earlier dream still echoing in the back of her mind like a half-forgotten memory. The queen's fiery resemblance felt too real to be a mere dream. And now, with Caelan's revelations, the pieces were falling into place.

Her mother had tried to unite the Courts of Snow and Ash, and it had destroyed her. Valira's stomach twisted at the thought. What if she made the same mistake? And brought nothing but ruin?

"Caelan," she began, her voice tentative as they continued through the snow. "Do you think my mother was wrong? Trying to unite the courts, I mean."

Caelan's expression was guarded, his gaze fixed ahead. "I don't know enough to say for certain. But if your mother believed she could control both fire and ice, it was more than just ambition. She must have had a reason."

Valira shivered, not from the cold, but from the weight of his words. "But she failed. She lost control of the power."

"Maybe," Caelan replied, his voice calm. "But we don't know what happened to her in the end. Maybe it wasn't her power that failed—maybe it was the courts themselves."

Valira frowned, her thoughts clouded with confusion. She had been so focused on suppressing her power, so terrified of what she might become, that she hadn't considered the possibility that her mother's failure wasn't entirely her fault. What if it was the courts that had driven her to destruction? What if this whole war, this endless conflict between fire and ice, was built on a foundation of fear and misunderstanding?

As they walked, Valira's thoughts drifted back to her dream—the vision of the fiery queen consumed by flames. She could still feel the heat from it, the overwhelming fire that had nearly burned her from the inside out. It wasn't just a memory; it was a warning.

"There has to be more to it," Valira muttered to herself, her brow furrowed.

Caelan shot her a sidelong glance. "What do you mean?"

"The dream I had... It felt like more than just a memory. Like there was something else my mother wanted me to see. Or something she wanted to tell me."

Caelan slowed his pace, his gaze sharp. "You think your mother is reaching out to you from beyond the grave?"

Valira hesitated, her pulse quickening. "I don't know. I can't ignore the sense that there's more to this, something I have to comprehend."

Caelan's jaw tightened, his expression unreadable. "If that's true, then we need to find answers. And quickly. The courts won't give us much time."

Valira nodded, her mind already racing ahead. Unsure where to begin, she couldn't uncover her mother's truth. But one thing was certain—her fate may mirror it. She could lose herself to the power inside her, just as her mother had.

They walked in silence, the snow crunching beneath their boots. Valira's thoughts were spinning, but she couldn't ignore the strange sense of urgency growing in her chest. She didn't just need to control the power within her—she needed to understand it. To understand why it existed, and what her mother had truly intended.

"We should rest soon," Caelan said after a while, glancing up at the sky, which was darkening as night approached. "The storm has passed, but the temperature will plummet once the sun goes down."

Valira nodded, though the idea of resting again so soon made her uneasy. Time felt like a luxury they couldn't afford, especially with the Ash Court still hunting them.

As they reached a small clearing, Caelan motioned for her to stop. The snow was deep here, but the thick canopy of trees blocked the worst of the wind. Caelan cleared a patch of ground for a fire, his movements quick and efficient.

Valira crouched beside him, watching as he worked. "You're pretty good at this," she said, trying to lighten the mood.

Caelan gave her a small, fleeting smile. "Survival isn't optional in the Snow Court."

Valira's heart ached at the reminder of the life he had left behind. He was risking everything by helping her—his duty, his loyalty to his kingdom, and perhaps even his life. And yet, here he was, fighting beside her, despite everything.

"I'm sorry," Valira said softly, her voice barely audible over the wind.

Caelan paused, his eyes flicking to hers in surprise. "For what?"

"For dragging you into this," she continued, her gaze dropping to the snow. "For putting you in a position where you have to choose between your kingdom and—"

"Don't," Caelan interrupted, his voice firm. "This was my choice. No one forced me to help you."

Valira looked up, meeting his gaze. There was a sincerity in his eyes that made her chest tighten. She didn't know what to say, didn't know how to express the gratitude—and guilt—she felt.

Before she could respond, a crack echoed through the trees, followed by the unmistakable sound of footsteps crunching snow.

Caelan was on his feet in an instant, his hand on the hilt of his sword, his eyes scanning the forest.

"They've found us," he muttered, his voice low and tense.

Valira's heart pounded in her chest as she stood, her body tensing. She could feel the fire stirring within her, the heat rising in her veins.

The Ash Court was closing in.

Valira's pulse quickened, the crack of footsteps echoing in the quiet forest as her heart thudded in her chest. Caelan stood tense beside her, his hand hovering over the hilt of his sword. The fire in her veins stirred, the heat simmering beneath her skin, warning her of the danger creeping closer.

She strained her ears, listening to the approach of their pursuers. Whoever it was, they were moving quickly—too quickly. Valira's breath caught as she realized they weren't alone anymore.

"Stay low," Caelan whispered, his voice tight as he crouched beside her. "We can't let them surround us."

Valira nodded, dropping to the ground, the cold snow soaking through her cloak. Her mind raced, her senses heightened by the growing tension. She could feel the heat rising inside her, the fire eager to escape, but she fought to keep it in check. This wasn't the time to lose control.

Caelan's eyes darted toward the trees, his expression hardening. "They're coming from both sides."

Panic flickered through Valira, but she forced

herself to stay calm. She couldn't afford to lose her head now. Not when they were so close.

"What do we do?" she whispered, her voice barely audible.

"We fight," Caelan replied, his tone resolute. He drew his sword, the blade gleaming in the fading light. "But we have to be smart. Stay behind me, and don't use your power unless you have no choice. They'll sense it."

Valira swallowed hard, her heart pounding in her chest. She knew he was right. The moment she unleashed her power, the Ash Court would know exactly where she was. But if they were outnumbered...

Before she could ponder further, the first figure entered the clearing, his silhouette outlined in the dim light. He wore the dark robes of the Ash Court, his face obscured by a hood, but Valira could see the faint glow of fire flickering at his fingertips.

The hunter.

Behind him, two more figures emerged from the trees, their eyes locked onto Valira and Caelan. Their movements were slow, deliberate, like predators stalking their prey.

Caelan tensed beside her, his grip on the sword tightening. "There's no way around this," he muttered under his breath. "When I move, follow my lead."

Valira's throat tightened, her hands trembling as she nodded. The fire inside her was flaring now, desperate to be set free. But she held it back, just as Caelan had warned. For now.

The lead hunter took a step forward, his hand raised, fire swirling in his palm. "The Ash Queen wants her alive," he called out, his voice cold and commanding. "But the prince... you're expendable."

Valira's heart leapt in her chest as the hunter hurled the fireball toward Caelan. The flames shot through the air, crackling with deadly heat, but Caelan was already moving. In a blur of motion, he raised his sword, deflecting the fire with a burst of icy energy that sent the flames scattering harmlessly to the ground.

The other two hunters lunged forward, their movements swift and precise. Valira gasped, her instincts kicking in as she stepped back, but Caelan was there, his sword flashing as he parried their attacks. Steel clashed with flame, the sound of battle filling the clearing as Caelan fought off the hunters with skill and precision.

Valira's breath came in ragged gasps as she watched, her body trembling with the effort of holding back the fire. She wanted to help him, to do something—anything—but Caelan's words echoed in her mind. *Don't use your power unless you have no choice.*

One of the hunters broke off from the fight, his gaze locked onto Valira. Her heart pounded in her ears as he approached, his hands ablaze with fire. She stepped back, her breath catching in her throat as he raised his hand, preparing to strike.

"I've got her," he hissed, his eyes narrowing with malice.

Time seemed to slow. Valira's pulse quickened, and the fire inside her flared, a surge of heat rushing through her veins. She couldn't hold it back anymore. Not this time.

With a desperate cry, Valira raised her hands, the fire bursting from her palms in a fiery arc. The hunter barely had time to react before the flames engulfed him; his scream pierced the air as he staggered back, consumed by the inferno.

Valira's chest heaved, her hands trembling as the fire receded. The air shimmered with heat, the snow beneath her feet melting into water. She had done it— she had controlled the fire. But at what cost?

Caelan turned, his eyes widening as he saw what she had done. "Valira, no!" he shouted, his voice filled with panic. "They'll know where we are!"

But it was too late. In the distance, Valira could already see more figures moving through the trees, drawn to the surge of power she had unleashed.

The Ash Court was coming. And now, they knew exactly where to find her.

Valira's heart pounded as she watched more hunters emerge from the shadows of the forest, their eyes glowing with the same fiery light. Her hands trembled, the remnants of heat from her attack still burning in her palms.

Caelan shot her a sharp look, his expression a mixture of frustration and fear. "We need to move, now!" he shouted, his voice cutting through the chaos.

Valira nodded, her pulse racing. But as she took a step back, she felt the heat in the air intensify, the ground beneath her feet growing warmer. The hunters were closing in, their movements swift and deliberate, fire swirling in their hands.

Panic surged through her. There were too many of them—more than she and Caelan could fight off on their own. She clenched her fists, the fire within her begging to be unleashed again, but she hesitated. The last time she'd used it, she had revealed their location. What if she made things worse?

"We'll never outrun them," Valira said breathlessly, her gaze flicking to the hunters. "They're too fast."

Caelan's jaw tightened as he scanned the clearing. "We don't need to outrun them," he muttered. "We just need to slow them down."

Before Valira could respond, Caelan turned toward the advancing hunters and raised his hand. A blast of icy wind erupted from his palm, spreading across the ground in a wave of frost. The snow hardened instantly;

the temperature plummeting as a sheet of ice formed beneath the hunters' feet. The nearest one slipped, crashing to the ground, his fire extinguished in a puff of steam.

"Run!" Caelan shouted, grabbing Valira's hand and pulling her toward the trees.

They sprinted into the forest, the cold air stinging Valira's face as they wove through the trees. Her heart hammered in her chest, her breath coming in ragged gasps. Behind them, she could hear the shouts of the hunters, their frustration echoing through the woods as they struggled to regain their footing.

But Valira knew it wouldn't last. They couldn't run forever.

Caelan pulled her along, his pace relentless. He didn't speak, his focus entirely on the path ahead. The trees grew denser, their branches forming a thick canopy overhead, blocking out what little light remained. With each step, the darkness deepened, turning the world into a realm of shadows and icy chill.

Finally, they reached a small clearing, and Caelan slowed, his breath heavy from exertion. Valira doubled over, trying to catch her breath, her lungs burning from the cold air.

"We can't keep this up," she gasped, her chest heaving. "They'll find us."

Caelan's expression was grim as he scanned the

surrounding forest. "I know," he said quietly. "But we have to keep moving. We're too close to give up now."

Valira frowned, wiping the sweat from her brow. "Too close to what?"

Caelan hesitated, his gaze flicking to her before he spoke. "There's someone who can help us. A contact I trust. If we can reach them before the Ash Court catches up, we might stand a chance."

Valira's heart sank. "Why didn't you tell me this before?"

"Because I wasn't sure if we'd make it this far," Caelan admitted, his voice low. "But now... we have no other choice."

Valira straightened, her mind racing. She didn't know if she could trust him, didn't know if this mysterious contact would be able to help, but they had no other options. The Ash Court was hunting her, and the Snow Court wanted her dead. Caelan was the only one standing between her and the forces that sought to destroy her.

"Okay," she said quietly. "Let's go."

They moved through the trees again, this time slower, more cautious. The sounds of pursuit had faded, but Valira knew it wouldn't be long before the hunters picked up their trail again. Every crack of a branch or rustle of leaves set her on edge, her nerves frayed from the constant tension.

As they pushed deeper into the forest, the air grew

colder, the snow beneath their feet crunching with every step. Valira shivered, pulling her cloak tighter around her shoulders, but the cold was a welcome relief compared to the heat that still simmered inside her. She had come so close to losing control, and the thought of what might have happened terrified her.

Caelan walked ahead, his posture tense, his eyes scanning the surroundings with practiced vigilance. He hadn't spoken much since they had fled the clearing, and Valira could feel the weight of unspoken words hanging between them. She wanted to ask him more about his contact, about what they would do once they reached safety, but she didn't have the energy to press him.

After what felt like hours, they finally reached the edge of the forest. Valira blinked against the sudden brightness as they stepped into an open field, the sun dipping low on the horizon, casting long shadows across the snow.

"There," Caelan said, pointing to a cluster of buildings in the distance. "We're almost there."

Valira squinted, her heart leaping with hope. It looked like a small village, nestled at the base of a mountain, smoke curling from the chimneys of a few houses. Relief washed over her—maybe they had a chance after all.

But before they could take another step, a loud crack split the air.

Valira whirled around, her breath catching in her throat. Standing at the edge of the forest, the hunters had found them, fire blazing in their hands.

The chase was over. They were cornered.

Valira's breath caught as she locked eyes with the lead hunter, his hand already raised, fire crackling at his fingertips. Caelan stepped in front of her, sword drawn. She could see the tension in his stance—there were too many of them, and they had nowhere left to run.

The hunters advanced slowly, their footsteps crunching through the snow, the flames in their hands casting flickering shadows across the field. Valira's pulse quickened, the fire in her chest surging with a mix of fear and desperation.

They had reached the village, but it didn't matter. The Ash Court wouldn't stop until they had her.

"We're out of time," Caelan muttered, his voice tight with frustration.

Valira's heart pounded in her chest. She couldn't let this happen. Not here. Not like this. She had to do something.

But what? If she unleashed the fire inside her, she risked losing control again. She risked becoming the very weapon the courts feared.

"Valira," Caelan said, his voice low and urgent. "You need to listen to me. You can't fight them all."

Her breath hitched as she looked at him, panic rising in her chest. "Then what do we do?"

Caelan's eyes darkened, a fierce determination flashing in his gaze. "You run. I'll hold them off."

Valira's heart froze. "No. You can't—"

"There's no other choice," Caelan interrupted, his tone sharp and urgent. "They want you. If I can buy you some time, you can make it to the village." He caught her gaze, his expression softening just slightly as he reached into his pocket, pulling out a small, weathered map and pressing it into her hands.

"Find the alley between the smithy and the baker's shop—it's narrow, with ivy crawling up the walls. Look for a door painted black with three iron studs shaped like a wolf's head. Knock twice, then once more after a pause. My contact's name is Lynel. They'll keep you safe, no matter what happens."

Valira glanced down at the map, her fingers tracing the faded ink. "Are you sure they'll help me?" she asked, her voice barely more than a whisper.

Caelan's gaze softened, and he nodded. "They owe me a life debt. They won't turn you away."

Valira shook her head, her voice breaking. "I'm not leaving you."

"You have to," Caelan said, his voice softer now. "You're the one who can end this. Not me."

Tears blurred Valira's vision as she looked at him, her chest aching with the weight of his words. She couldn't lose him—not now, not after everything they had been through.

But before she could say anything more, the hunters moved in, their flames roaring to life.

Caelan stepped forward, his sword gleaming in the dying light.

And Valira ran.

CHAPTER 3

SECRETS OF THE PAST

V alira's feet pounded against the snow-covered ground, her heart hammering in her chest as she fled toward the village. The cold air bit at her skin, but she barely felt it—the fire inside her was raging, the heat building with every step. Caelan's words echoed in her mind: You run. I'll hold them off.

The village loomed ahead, its silhouette dark against the snow-covered field, but every step she took felt like a betrayal. She didn't want to leave him, didn't want to abandon the only person who had stood by her, even when he had every reason not to. But what other choice did she have? If she stayed, they would both die.

The sound of clashing steel and roaring flames filled the air behind her, and Valira's chest tightened as she imagined Caelan fighting off the hunters alone. She had to make it to the village, had to find his contact—but the guilt gnawed at her, threatening to pull her back.

Suddenly, a sharp pain stabbed through her chest, and she stumbled, gasping for breath. The fire inside her flared violently, burning hotter than ever before. Valira's hands shook as she pressed them to her chest, trying to contain the power threatening to escape.

No... not now, she thought desperately. She couldn't lose control again—not here, not with Caelan's life hanging in the balance.

But the fire wouldn't be denied. It surged within her, a relentless force that demanded to be unleashed. Valira's vision blurred as she collapsed to her knees, the snow melting beneath her as flames flickered at her fingertips.

"I can't..." she whispered, her voice trembling. "I can't control it."

The fire grew hotter, and for a moment, Valira was certain it would consume her completely. But then, through the haze of heat, she felt something else—a cold, steady presence, like a hand reaching through the flames.

Caelan.

Her breath caught as she realized what was happening. He was still fighting, still out there, risking everything for her. She couldn't let him die. She couldn't let this power destroy them both.

With a shaky breath, Valira forced herself to stand,

the fire still raging inside her. She couldn't hold it back any longer. The hunters were too close, and Caelan was outnumbered. She had no choice.

Her hands began to glow, the heat radiating from her palms as she turned back toward the forest. Flames flickered, and she clenched her fists, forcing the power to bend to her will.

She wasn't going to run anymore.

Valira took a deep breath, the fire within her roaring to life, and she let it loose.

A wave of flame shot out from her hands, scorching the snow and illuminating the darkening sky with a brilliant glow. The power surged through her veins, hotter and stronger than ever before, but this time, she wasn't afraid.

She was in control.

The hunters halted, their eyes wide with shock as they saw the firestorm sweeping toward them. Caelan stood in the center of the battlefield, his sword raised, ice shimmering at his feet. His gaze locked onto hers, and for a moment, their eyes met—fire and ice, balanced in perfect harmony.

And then, the flames reached the hunters.

The air crackled with heat as the fire engulfed them, their screams lost in the roar of the inferno. Valira watched, her chest heaving, as the flames consumed everything in their path. The power within her was a force of destruction, but for the first time, she had wielded it with purpose.

The flames flickered and died, leaving nothing but ash in their wake. The hunters were gone, reduced to nothing more than charred shadows on the snow.

Valira stood trembling, her hands still warm from the fire, her breath ragged. The power had drained her, but she was still standing. She had done it.

Caelan approached her slowly, his sword lowered, his expression unreadable. For a long moment, neither of them spoke. The village was quiet, the snow falling softly, the only sound the distant crackle of dying flames.

"You came back," Caelan said quietly, his voice filled with a mixture of surprise and something else—something Valira couldn't quite name.

She nodded, her throat tight. "I couldn't leave you."

Caelan's eyes softened, and for a moment, the weight of everything they had been through seemed to lift. They had survived, but the fight wasn't over. The Ash Court would send more hunters, and the Snow Court would still see her as a threat.

But for now, they had each other.

Valira took a deep breath, the fire inside her finally quiet, and met Caelan's gaze. "What now?"

Caelan glanced toward the village, his expression serious. "We find my contact. And then, we figure out how to end this war—once and for all."

Valira nodded, a glimmer of hope settling over her. The path ahead was uncertain, but for the first time, they weren't running anymore. They were ready to fight.

The village loomed closer, its chimneys sending thin wisps of smoke into the darkening sky. Valira and Caelan moved through the last stretch of the snow-covered field in silence, the tension between them still palpable. The flickering warmth of firelight from the village was a welcome sight, but Valira knew the hardest part of their journey was still ahead.

Her heart was heavy, the weight of what had just happened pressing down on her chest. She had unleashed her power again—this time fully, without restraint—and while it had saved them, the destruction it had left behind was undeniable. She could still feel the heat in her veins, like embers slowly burning beneath her skin. She wasn't sure if she could control it again.

They reached the edge of the village, where the first few buildings were huddled at the base of a towering mountain. The stone cottages were old and weathered, their windows glowing with the soft light of fires inside. The people here lived on the fringes of the courts' conflicts, far enough from the Ash and Snow Kingdoms to avoid most of the fighting—but not far enough to escape the growing shadow of war.

Caelan slowed his pace, his eyes scanning the narrow alleyways between the cottages. "We need to be careful," he murmured. "Not everyone here is friendly to strangers."

Valira nodded, though her mind was elsewhere. She couldn't shake the memory of the fire she had unleashed, couldn't forget the look in Caelan's eyes when he saw what she was capable of. He had trusted her to run, and instead, she had turned back and used the very thing he feared.

They wound their way through the village, keeping to the shadows as they approached a larger building near the center of the settlement. Caelan led the way, his posture tense, his hand resting on the hilt of his sword.

"This is it," he said quietly as they reached the building. "My contact lives here. They'll help us."

Valira's pulse quickened. She wasn't sure what she had expected, but the building in front of her looked no different from the other cottages—small, modest, with smoke curling from the chimney. But if Caelan believed this person could help, then she had no choice but to trust him.

Caelan knocked on the door, his hand still resting on his sword, just in case. For a long moment, there was no response, and Valira's heart began to race, fear creeping in. What if this contact had turned against them? What if the Ash Court had already found them?

Just as Valira was about to speak, the door creaked open, revealing a tall figure cloaked in dark furs. The person's face was shadowed, their features obscured, but their eyes gleamed with sharp intelligence.

"Caelan," the figure said, their voice low and calm. "You're late."

Caelan let out a frosty breath. "We ran into some trouble," he replied, glancing over his shoulder. "But we made it."

The figure stepped aside, gesturing for them to enter. "Come inside. Quickly."

Valira hesitated for only a moment before following Caelan into the small cottage. The interior was warm, the air filled with the scent of burning wood and herbs. The fire crackled in the hearth, casting flickering shadows across the stone walls. It felt like a different world from the frozen wasteland they had just left behind.

The figure closed the door behind them and pulled back their hood, revealing a woman with sharp features and silver hair. Her eyes were calculating, taking in every detail of Valira and Caelan with a quick glance.

"This is her, then?" the woman, Lynel, asked, her gaze settling on Valira.

Caelan nodded. "Yes. Valira."

Lynel's eyes narrowed slightly as she looked Valira

up and down, as if measuring her worth. "You've made quite the impression already," she said dryly. "The Ash Court is in chaos over what happened in the forest."

Valira's heart skipped a beat. "How do you know?"

Lynel smiled, a cold, knowing smile. "I hear things. And in times like these, news travels fast."

Valira's mind raced, her thoughts swirling with questions. Who was this woman? How did she know so much about the Ash Court? And more importantly—what was her connection to Caelan?

Lynel moved to the hearth, stirring the fire with a metal poker before turning back to them. "You're in danger, Valira. More than you realize."

Valira swallowed hard, her throat tight. "I know that. The Ash Court won't stop hunting me."

"It's not just the Ash Court," Lynel replied, her voice steady. "The Snow Court is watching, too. They know you're powerful. And they're afraid."

Caelan shifted beside her, his posture tense. "That's why we came to you. We need your help."

Lynel studied them both for a long moment before nodding. "You've come to the right place. But what you're asking for won't be easy."

Valira frowned, confusion clouding her mind. "What are we asking for?"

Lynel's gaze flicked to Caelan, who remained silent, his expression unreadable. Then she looked back at Valira, her eyes sharp as ice. "You want to end the war, don't you? To stop the courts from tearing each other apart?"

Valira's heart raced. "Yes, but—how?"

Lynel's expression hardened. "You have to understand, Valira, the fire inside you isn't just a weapon. It's part of something much larger. Something that has been building for generations."

Valira's breath caught, her pulse quickening. "What do you mean?"

Lynel stepped closer, her eyes gleaming with a cold intensity. "You're not the first to possess both fire and ice. Your mother—she tried to unite the courts, but she failed. She didn't understand the full extent of her power. But you... you have the chance to finish what she started."

Valira's mind reeled. She had known her mother's legacy was tied to the courts, but this... it was too much. Too overwhelming.

"I don't even know how to control it," she whispered, her voice trembling. "How am I supposed to finish what she couldn't?"

Lynel's gaze softened, just slightly. "You'll learn. With Caelan's help, and mine, you'll learn to control both fire and ice. But you need to be prepared. The courts won't give up their power without a fight."

Valira's heart pounded in her chest, fear and hope warring within her. She had come so far, fought so hard, and yet the path ahead seemed more uncertain than ever. But there was no turning back now. She had to find a way to control the power inside her—for herself, for Caelan, and for the future of both courts.

"I'm ready," Valira said quietly, her voice steady despite the fear in her chest.

Lynel smiled, a small, cold smile. "Good. Then we begin."

The small room within the cottage grew even quieter after Lynel's declaration. Valira's heart still pounded in her chest, the weight of what she had agreed to sinking deeper into her bones. Control both fire and ice? Finish what her mother had started? It all seemed impossible, but she had no choice. She had to find a way.

Lynel watched her with those piercing silver eyes, as if she could see the doubt creeping into Valira's thoughts. "This won't be easy," she said, her tone serious but not unkind. "The courts have spent centuries locked in their ways, afraid of the balance you represent. But I've trained others before you. None like you, of course, but enough to know that power can be mastered."

Valira swallowed hard, glancing over at Caelan. He hadn't said much since they entered the cottage, his usual stoic demeanor only growing more impenetrable. But there was a tension in him she hadn't noticed before, something tight around the corners of his eyes. He wasn't unaffected by what they were about to face.

"You've trained others?" Valira asked, trying to focus on the woman, trying to grasp what lay ahead.

"Yes," the woman replied, crossing her arms. "Though most were gifted in one element, not two. Fire alone is a difficult force to tame. The raw destruction it craves... most people are consumed by it long before they learn to control it. But you—you have the advantage of balance. Ice can temper fire, just as fire can awaken the stillness of ice."

Valira furrowed her brow, trying to make sense of the Lynel's words. The fire inside her had never felt balanced. It had always been overwhelming, pushing to the surface no matter how hard she tried to suppress it. And the ice... well, that still felt foreign to her, a power she hadn't fully tapped into yet.

"How do I balance them?" Valira asked, her voice soft but filled with urgency. "Every time I've tried to control the fire, it... it's like it wants to consume everything. And the ice—it only came when I was scared. I don't know how to bring it out."

Lynel studied her for a moment, then motioned toward the hearth, where the flames burned brightly. "Sit," she said. "Let's begin with the fire."

Valira hesitated but did as she was told, lowering herself onto the stone floor in front of the fire. The heat from the flames danced across her skin, and almost immediately, she felt the familiar stir of warmth inside her chest; the fire that simmered just beneath the surface.

Lynel crouched beside her, her silver hair catching the firelight. "Fire is an element of emotion," she said quietly. "It feeds off passion, anger, fear—anything that burns inside you. The more you resist it, the more it grows out of control. You have to learn to feel the fire, but not let it consume you."

Valira frowned. "How do I do that?"

"Start small," Lynel instructed, her tone patient. "Feel the heat, but don't let it overwhelm you. Imagine it like a flame in your hand—small, controlled. Not a wildfire. Not a weapon."

Valira took a deep breath, closing her eyes. She could feel the heat in her chest, a simmering warmth that was always there, waiting. She imagined it as a tiny flame, cupped in her palm, like a flickering candle. Her heart pounded as she focused on keeping it small, keeping it from spreading.

At first, it was easy. The flame was contained, a gentle warmth in her chest. But then, as she felt the power swirling within her, the heat began to grow, pushing against the edges of her control. It wanted out.

"Breathe," Lynel said softly. "You control the flame. It doesn't control you."

Valira clenched her fists, trying to force the fire back down, but it surged forward, desperate to be unleashed.

Her breathing quickened, panic rising in her throat. She couldn't do it. It was too much.

The fire burst from her hands, a flash of heat that sent sparks flying into the air. Valira gasped, pulling her hands back as the flames danced wildly in the hearth. She had lost control again.

Lynel sighed, standing up slowly. "It will take time," she said, her voice calm despite the setback. "You're trying to force it, instead of letting the fire move with you. You'll learn."

Valira felt her shoulders slump, the weight of her failure heavy in her chest. She had thought she was making progress, but this... this was harder than she had imagined.

Caelan stepped forward, his expression unreadable. "She'll get there," he said quietly, more to himself than to the woman. "She just needs time."

The woman nodded, her gaze softening slightly. "You have potential, Valira. Don't lose hope. You've already survived what many couldn't. That alone proves you're stronger than you think."

Valira looked up at her, a flicker of determination sparking in her chest. She couldn't give up—not now. Not when so much was at stake.

"I won't," she said softly, her voice filled with resolve. "I'll keep trying."

Lynel's lips curved into a small smile. "Good. We'll

continue with ice tomorrow. But for now, rest. You'll need your strength."

Valira nodded, though her mind was still spinning. Control both fire and ice? She didn't know if she could. But she had to try. For her mother's legacy. For Caelan. For herself.

As the fire crackled beside her, Valira leaned back, her thoughts swirling like embers in the wind.

———

The night was long and Valira tossed and turned, her mind unable to settle. Every time she closed her eyes, the memory of the fire exploding from her hands flashed behind her lids, a reminder of how quickly everything could go wrong. She had thought she was gaining control, but the fire seemed determined to prove her wrong. Now, with the prospect of learning ice the next day, her nerves twisted even tighter.

Would it be the same? Would the cold within her spiral out of control just like the fire? Or worse, would it remain buried, unreachable when she needed it most?

She finally drifted into a fitful sleep, filled with dreams of burning forests and freezing winds, her mother's voice calling her name through the flames, then through a haze of ice.

When she woke, the cottage was still dim, the embers in the hearth barely glowing. Caelan was sitting near the door, his eyes half-lidded but alert, his body tense even in rest. He must have been watching over her, keeping the night's dangers at bay.

Valira pushed herself up slowly, blinking away the remnants of her dreams. She knew today would be no easier than yesterday, but there was no choice but to keep going. If she didn't learn to control her powers, they wouldn't survive much longer. She couldn't keep relying on Caelan to save her. She had to be stronger.

Just as she stood, Lynel entered from the back room, her expression unreadable, but her silver eyes sharp as ever. "You're awake. Good," she said, glancing briefly at Caelan before focusing entirely on Valira. "We don't have time to waste today. Come. We start now."

Valira nodded, pulling her cloak tightly around her as she followed Lynel out into the cold morning air. Caelan stood and moved to follow, but the woman raised a hand to stop him. "She needs to do this alone."

Caelan frowned, but after a moment, he gave a slight nod and stepped back, watching Valira with a mixture of concern and something else—something unspoken.

Valira met his gaze briefly, then turned and followed Lynel into the snow-covered clearing just outside the village. The cold hit her immediately, sharp and biting, but instead of retreating from it, she let it in. Lynel's words from the day before echoed in her mind: *The cold is already in you. You just have to let it out.*

Once they reached the center of the clearing, Lynel

stopped and turned to face her. "Today, you learn ice," she said, her voice as steady and cold as the frigid air. "You've already felt it, haven't you? The way it calms you, sharpens your focus. Fire is chaos, but ice is clarity."

Valira nodded, though her heart was pounding. She had felt the ice inside her before, but it had only come in moments of fear or desperation, never by her choice. And when it had appeared, it was always fleeting, like a distant memory she couldn't quite hold on to.

"How do I call it?" Valira asked, her voice quieter than she intended. The fire had always been there, ready to burst out whenever she lost control, but the ice... it felt like something buried deep within her, hidden beneath layers of doubt and fear.

"By accepting the cold," Lynel replied, her eyes narrowing slightly. "You're afraid of your fire, and that fear keeps the ice locked away. Let go of your fear. Let the cold in."

Valira swallowed hard, her breath fogging in the frigid air. She closed her eyes, trying to focus on the cold —the way it prickled her skin, the way it stung her lungs when she breathed in too deeply. She imagined that cold sinking into her, freezing away the uncertainty and fear.

At first, there was nothing. Just the usual chill of the morning air pressing against her skin. But then, slowly, she felt something stir deep inside her. A familiar sharpness, like the edge of a blade. The cold began to spread through her veins, steady and precise, pushing aside the warmth of the fire.

"Good," Lynel said, her voice calm but firm. "Now, don't force it. Let the cold flow through you, but don't try to control it yet. Just feel it."

Valira took a deep breath, focusing on the sensation of the ice spreading through her. It wasn't like the fire, wild and consuming. The ice was quiet, deliberate. It moved with purpose, chilling her blood but leaving her mind clear, sharper than it had been in days.

She opened her eyes, and to her surprise, frost had formed a crust on the ground. The snow at her feet was glittering with delicate ice crystals, spiraling out from where she stood. Her breath caught in her throat, but she didn't let the surprise break her concentration.

Lynel smiled faintly, the first sign of approval Valira had seen. "Good. You're starting to understand. But this is just the beginning."

Valira's heart raced, her mind spinning with a mix of excitement and fear. She had felt the ice, had controlled it—at least for now. But she knew this was only the surface of what she was capable of. And she also knew that if she lost focus for even a moment, the balance between fire and ice could shatter, leaving her at the mercy of both elements.

Lynel stepped forward, her silver eyes gleaming. "There is more inside you, Valira. More than you know.

But you must learn to balance the two—fire and ice. If you don't, one will consume you. And it won't be gentle."

Valira's pulse quickened as the weight of her words settled over her. Balance. It was something she had never truly known, not with her powers, not with her emotions. But if she wanted to survive—if she wanted to end this war—she had to find that balance.

"I'm ready," she said softly, though the fear still gnawed at her.

Lynel nodded, her smile fading as her expression turned serious once more. "We'll see."

Valira took a deep breath, the cold air filling her lungs. The fire within her stirred, but she pushed it down, letting the ice rise instead, calm and steady. She didn't know what the future held, but for now, she had taken the first step toward controlling the power inside her.

The ice lingered at Valira's fingertips, a soft, humming energy that contrasted sharply with the chaos of fire she had grown so used to. Lynel's sharp eyes followed her every move, judging silently as Valira stood in the snow-covered clearing, her breath forming soft clouds in the air. For a moment, she felt the calm Lynel had spoken of

—the clarity, the precision of the cold coursing through her.

But as Valira stood in the growing quiet, something else began to stir within her. Deep in her chest, the familiar heat of the fire rumbled awake. It pushed against the cold, like two opposing forces battling for control.

"Stay focused," Lynel said, her voice cutting through the tension.

Valira gritted her teeth, trying to ignore the fire. She wanted to keep the ice, to let it guide her, but the warmth was building, insistent, as though it sensed its rival. Her fingers trembled, and the ice that had so carefully crystallized beneath her began to melt, the sharpness of it retreating as the fire grew stronger.

"I can't," Valira whispered, shaking her head. "It's too much."

"Don't fight it," Lynel commanded, her tone as icy as ever. "You cannot deny one without weakening the other. Let the fire rise, but do not lose yourself to it."

Valira swallowed hard, fear clawing at her chest. Let the fire rise? She had spent her life trying to push it down, to keep it from consuming everything in its path. How could she possibly let it free now?

But the Lynel's words echoed in her mind: *You cannot deny one without weakening the other.*

With a deep, shaky breath, Valira loosened her grip on the ice, allowing the fire to unfurl within her. The heat rose quickly, spreading through her veins, fierce and wild. It surged to the surface, battling with the cold, and for a terrifying moment, Valira thought she might lose control completely.

"Valira." Caelan's voice came from behind her, steady and sure. "You can do this."

His presence was like an anchor, pulling her back from the edge of panic. Valira took another breath, forcing herself to focus. The fire roared, but she didn't let it overwhelm her. Instead, she tried to let the ice rise alongside it, not in opposition, but rather in balance.

At first, it was like trying to walk a tightrope in a storm. The fire pushed, the ice pulled, and Valira struggled to maintain her footing between the two. Her breath came in sharp gasps, her body trembling with the effort. But slowly, slowly, she began to find a rhythm.

The snow around her feet melted, but it didn't turn to steam. Instead, the water froze again, forming delicate patterns in the air, the fire and ice dancing together in a strange, beautiful harmony. Valira stared in awe as the energy flowed through her, not wild and chaotic, but controlled, balanced.

"You're doing it," Caelan said softly, his voice filled with something like wonder.

Valira's heart raced, but this time, it wasn't from fear. She had done it. She had found the balance.

Lynel nodded, her expression approving but still

guarded. "You've taken the first step," she said. "But this is just the beginning. There will be moments when the balance will slip, when one will try to overpower the other. You must remain vigilant."

Valira let out a breath she hadn't realized she was holding, the fire and ice still swirling inside her, but no longer threatening to consume her. She had taken control—if only for a moment.

"I didn't think it was possible," Valira murmured, her voice quiet with awe. "I never thought they could exist together."

Lynel's gaze softened slightly, though her tone remained sharp. "It is possible. You are proof of that. But do not grow complacent. There are many who will try to use you for this power."

Valira nodded, her heart sinking as the weight of Lynel's warning settled over her. The courts—the Ash and Snow—would never stop hunting her. They would want this power for themselves, and they would do whatever it took to claim it.

Caelan stepped closer, his presence a steadying force beside her. "You did it, Valira," he said, his voice low. "You found the balance. Now we can move forward."

Valira glanced up at him, her heart lifting slightly at the determination in his eyes. She had succeeded in this first step, but the road ahead was still uncertain, still filled with danger. The courts wouldn't give up their pursuit, and the threat of war loomed closer with every passing day.

But for the first time, Valira didn't feel like a victim of her powers. She wasn't just the Ash Princess or the Snow Court's target. She was something more. Something stronger.

"We can't stay here much longer," Caelan said, turning to Lynel. "What's next?"

Lynel's expression grew serious again, her silver eyes narrowing. "The balance you've found is fragile. The fire and ice will always try to tear you apart. To master them, you'll need to face what lies in your past—and the war that's coming."

Valira's breath caught. "What do you mean? Face my past?"

Lynel glanced toward the mountains in the distance, her gaze darkening. "You cannot control these powers without understanding where they came from. There are secrets buried in the courts—secrets about your family, about the curse that binds fire and ice. To break it, you must return to where it all began."

Valira's pulse quickened. "Where?"

Lynel turned back to her, her expression unreadable. "The Court of Ash."

Valira's heart dropped into her stomach. The Court of Ash? The very place that wanted her dead?

She glanced at Caelan, panic flashing in her eyes. He

held her gaze, his expression steady, but she could see the worry beneath it.

"We can't go back there," Valira said, her voice trembling. "They'll kill me."

Lynel's eyes gleamed with cold certainty. "If you want to survive this, if you want to master your power, you'll have to face them. There is no other way."

Valira's mind raced, fear creeping into her chest. She wasn't ready for this. She had barely found the balance between fire and ice. How could she possibly face the Court of Ash?

But deep down, she knew Lynel was right. The answers she sought—the key to controlling her powers —lay in her past. And the only way forward was to confront it.

"We'll go," Caelan said, his voice quiet but firm. "But we'll do it on our terms."

Valira looked at him, her heart pounding. She didn't know how they would survive what lay ahead, but she knew one thing for certain: they couldn't run any longer.

The time had come to face the fire.

CHAPTER 4

FACING THE FLAMES

The gates of the Ash Court loomed ahead, dark and foreboding. Valira's heart pounded as they drew closer, each step heavier than the last. The ground beneath her feet had changed—no longer the soft, cold blanket of snow but the hard, cracked earth of the Ash Court's domain. Even the air felt different here, thick with heat and the scent of burning wood.

Caelan walked beside her, his face a mask of determination, though Valira could sense the tension in him. They were entering enemy territory. Returning to the place that had once branded her a threat, a weapon of destruction.

"How close are we?" Valira asked, her voice tight with anxiety.

Caelan glanced at her, his jaw clenched. "Too close

for comfort. We'll be in the heart of the Ash Court soon."

Valira's stomach twisted. She had only been a child the last time she was here, but the memories still lingered—fragments of fire and fear. Now, she was walking straight into the heart of that fear, seeking answers about her powers, about her mother's legacy.

"Do you think they know?" she asked quietly.

Caelan's eyes darkened. "They'll know soon enough. But we can't let them catch us off guard."

Valira nodded, but her heart was racing. The fire inside her stirred, reacting to the heat of the Ash Court. She had only just begun to balance the fire and ice, and already, she felt that balance slipping.

As they slipped through the outer gates, sticking to the shadows, Valira's eyes darted nervously to the patrols marching along the walls. The soldiers wore blackened armor, their faces hidden behind masks of ash and soot. Every step closer made Valira's pulse quicken, her skin prickling with unease.

"We can't be seen," Caelan muttered, his voice barely above a whisper. "If they recognize you, we're finished."

Valira nodded, pulling the hood of her cloak lower over her face. Her mother's blood ran through her veins, and if the Ash Court knew who she was, they would not hesitate to drag her back into their clutches.

As they moved deeper into the city, the streets grew narrower, lined with dark stone buildings that rose high above them. The air was thick with smoke, and every breath felt like it burned her lungs. Valira's heart raced, her hands trembling as she fought to keep her powers in check.

They turned a corner, slipping into a narrow alleyway, and came face-to-face with a figure cloaked in shadows.

Valira froze. Her first instinct was to reach for her powers, but Caelan's hand on her arm stopped her.

The figure stepped forward, revealing a familiar face. "I thought you might return," the woman said, her voice low and dangerous. "You've been expected."

Valira's breath caught in her throat as she recognized the woman standing before her. It was Alyssia, one of the Ash Court's most feared hunters. Her fiery hair matched the blaze of the Court itself, and her sharp eyes gleamed with a knowing look that sent a chill down Valira's spine.

"We didn't come here for a fight," Caelan said, his voice steady but edged with caution.

Alyssia smiled, a slow, dangerous smile. "You didn't come here to fight? Then why, pray tell, have you returned to the Court of Ash?"

Valira's stomach twisted. She had known the

journey back here would be dangerous, but seeing Alyssia brought it all crashing down around her. The Court hadn't forgotten her—hadn't forgotten the power she carried within her.

"We need answers," Valira said, stepping forward despite the fear gripping her heart. "About my mother. About what she was trying to do."

Alyssia's smile faded, her eyes narrowing as she studied Valira more closely. "Your mother's secrets are dangerous things. You shouldn't go digging where the fire runs deep."

"Please," Valira said, her voice trembling but determined. "I need to understand. I need to know why the Ash Court fears me."

Alyssia's gaze flicked to Caelan, then back to Valira. For a long moment, there was silence, the air between them thick with tension.

"Very well," Alyssia said at last, her tone cold. "But know this, child of fire: if you dig too deep, you might not like what you find."

Alyssia led them through the winding streets of the Ash Court, deeper into the heart of the city. The heat grew more intense with every step, and Valira felt the fire inside her stirring, rising to meet the flames of the city.

It was as if the very air was pulling the power from her, feeding the flames that lay dormant in her chest.

"You feel it, don't you?" Alyssia said, glancing back at Valira as they walked. "The fire of the Ash Court calls to you. It knows who you are."

Valira swallowed hard. "Yes, I feel it," she admitted. "But I don't understand it. My powers... they're unstable."

Alyssia smiled, but there was no warmth in it. "That's because you're trying to control something that cannot be controlled. Fire is chaos. It burns, it destroys, and it will consume you if you let it."

Valira's heart pounded. She had always known the fire was dangerous, had always feared the power that lurked inside her. But hearing Alyssia speak of it so coldly, as though it were inevitable that the fire would consume her, sent a wave of dread through her.

"Then how did my mother control it?" Valira asked, her voice barely above a whisper.

Alyssia's eyes darkened. "Your mother didn't control it. She thought she could, but in the end, it was the fire that controlled her."

Valira's stomach dropped. Was that her fate, too? To be consumed by the very power she was trying to master?

They finally reached a tall, imposing building at the center of the Ash Court. Alyssia stopped at the base of the steps, turning to face Valira and Caelan with a look of grim determination.

"This is where it all began," she said, her voice low. "Your mother's experiments, her attempts to unite fire and ice—it all started here."

Valira's breath caught. This place, this dark, foreboding building, held the answers she had been searching for. But it also held the weight of her mother's failures, the legacy of a power that had nearly torn the courts apart.

Alyssia stepped closer, her voice dropping to a whisper. "You want answers? You'll find them here. But know this, Valira—if you walk through those doors, there's no turning back. The Ash Court will not forgive another failure."

Valira glanced at Caelan, her heart pounding in her chest. She had come so far, but the fear of what she might find inside threatened to paralyze her. Was she ready for the truth? Could she handle the secrets buried within these walls?

"We don't have a choice," Caelan said softly, his eyes locked on hers. "We need to know."

Valira took a deep breath, her hands trembling as she looked up at the towering building before her. The fire inside her flared, the heat rising in response to the looming danger.

"We go in," Valira said, her voice steady despite the fear coursing through her.

And with that, they stepped forward, crossing the threshold into the heart of the Ash Court.

CHAPTER 5

INTO THE HEART OF FIRE

The doors to the Ash Court's heart closed behind them with a heavy thud, the sound echoing through the vast, dark hall. The temperature inside was stifling, the heat clinging to Valira's skin as if the very air was alive with fire. Her heart raced as she stepped forward, each step taking her deeper into the place that held the secrets of her mother's past—and, perhaps, her own fate.

Caelan walked silently beside her, his eyes scanning their surroundings, alert to any danger that might lurk in the shadows. Alyssia had stayed behind, her parting words still ringing in Valira's ears: *If you walk through those doors, there's no turning back.*

The truth felt heavy, like a weight pressing down on Valira's chest. This was where her mother's attempts to unite fire and ice had failed. And now, it was Valira's turn to face those same challenges. The fire within her stirred, as if sensing the significance of this place, while the cold of the ice stayed carefully dormant, balanced but distant.

"What do you think we'll find here?" Valira whispered, her voice barely audible in the oppressive silence.

Caelan shook his head, his jaw tense. "Answers, I hope. But we need to be careful. The Ash Court doesn't give up its secrets easily."

They moved deeper into the hall their footsteps muffled by the thick stone floor. The walls were adorned with tapestries depicting scenes of fire—battlefields consumed by flame, cities reduced to ash. Each one felt like a warning, a reminder of the power Valira carried within her.

The hall opened up into a grand chamber, its ceiling high and vaulted, flames dancing in sconces along the walls. At the center of the room was a large stone altar, blackened and cracked with age. Valira's breath caught in her throat as she realized what it was.

"This is where it happened," she whispered, her voice trembling. "This is where my mother..."

Her words trailed off as she stepped closer to the altar, the heat rising around her in waves. She could almost feel the echoes of the past, the fiery magic that had once pulsed through this place. The fire inside her responded, flaring in her chest, but Valira forced it down, struggling to maintain control.

Caelan stood beside her, his hand resting on the hilt of his sword as he studied the altar. "Do you think there's anything left here? Any clue about what she was trying to do?"

Valira shook her head, though the fear in her chest only grew. "I don't know. But we have to try." She stepped closer to the altar, her eyes scanning the intricate carvings that lined its surface. Symbols of fire and flame were etched deep into the stone, but there was something else, too—something hidden beneath the surface.

She reached out, her fingers brushing against the cold stone. The moment she made contact, a sharp pain shot through her hand, and she gasped, pulling back. The fire inside her surged, as if awakened by the touch, but the ice remained still, unreachable.

"What is it?" Caelan asked, stepping closer.

Valira shook her head, her heart racing. "I don't know. There's something... wrong. It feels like the fire wants to come out, but the ice—"

Before she could finish her sentence, a low rumbling sound filled the chamber, and the floor beneath them began to tremble. Valira stumbled back, her pulse quickening as the ground shifted, the altar cracking open with a sudden, violent force.

"Get back!" Caelan shouted, grabbing her arm and pulling her away from the altar as a blast of heat erupted from the ground, filling the room with a blinding light.

Valira shielded her eyes, her breath coming in short gasps as the heat washed over her. When the light faded, she looked up, her heart pounding. The altar had been split in two, and where it had once stood was now a glowing pit, the air around it shimmering with heat.

But it wasn't just heat. There was something else in the air, something ancient and powerful, and Valira could feel it pulling at her, drawing her closer.

"There's magic here," she whispered, her voice trembling. "Old magic."

Caelan frowned, his hand still on his sword. "What kind of magic?"

Valira shook her head, her heart pounding. "I don't know. But it's connected to the fire inside me."

She stepped forward, her hands trembling as she reached out toward the pit. The fire inside her responded, flaring in her chest, eager to meet the power that lay just beneath the surface.

"I have to touch it," she said, her voice barely above a whisper.

Caelan grabbed her arm, his grip firm. "Valira, no. You don't know what it will do."

She looked up at him, her heart racing. "I have to. It's the only way to understand what happened here."

Caelan hesitated, his eyes filled with worry, but after a long moment, he released her arm, stepping back.

Valira took a deep breath, her pulse quickening as she reached out toward the glowing pit. The heat was intense, but the fire inside her burned even hotter. She closed her eyes, letting the power flow through her, and the moment her fingers touched the edge of the pit, a wave of energy surged through her, filling her with a blinding heat.

Her eyes flew open as the power flooded her veins, the fire roaring to life inside her. But it wasn't just fire. There was something else—something darker, something colder. The ice.

For the first time, the two forces weren't at odds. They moved together, swirling inside her like a storm, filling her with a power she had never known before. Energy surged through Valira, fire and ice colliding but not battling. Instead, they twined together, forming a perfect harmony inside her. For a moment, she felt invincible, as though the power inside her could burn and freeze the world all at once. It was intoxicating, overwhelming, and terrifying.

But then, just as suddenly, the power began to recede. The flames around the altar dimmed, and the ground stopped shaking. Valira's knees buckled, and she collapsed, her body trembling with the aftershocks of the magic that had surged through her.

Caelan was at her side in an instant, his hand on her shoulder. "Valira? Are you okay?"

She nodded weakly, her breath coming in shallow gasps. "I... I don't know what that was."

"It looked like you were being consumed by the fire," Caelan said, his voice filled with concern. "But then—"

"It wasn't just fire," Valira interrupted, her voice shaky. "It was ice, too. They were... balanced."

Caelan frowned, helping her to her feet. "Balanced?"

Valira nodded, her mind still reeling from the experience. "I've never felt anything like it. It was like the fire and ice were working together, not fighting against each other."

Caelan's gaze darkened. "That's dangerous, Valira. You don't know what that power could do."

"I know," she said softly, her eyes drifting back to the altar. "But I think it's what my mother was trying to do. She wanted to unite the elements, to control both fire and ice."

Caelan's jaw clenched. "And look what happened to her."

Valira's heart sank. He was right. Her mother had tried to control both, and in the end, it had destroyed her. Was she walking down the same path?

Before she could dwell on the thought, a sound echoed through the chamber—the sound of footsteps approaching from the shadows. Valira's pulse quickened, and she turned toward the sound, her hand instinctively reaching for her power.

Out of the darkness stepped a figure.

"Alyssia," Caelan muttered, his hand tightening on his sword.

Alyssia smiled, her fiery hair gleaming in the dim light. "You've done it, haven't you? You've touched the magic."

Valira swallowed hard, her body still trembling with the remnants of the power. "What are you doing here?"

"I had to see it for myself," Alyssia said, stepping closer. "The magic that was locked away, the power your mother tried to control. I had to know if you could unlock it."

Valira's heart raced. "Why?"

Alyssia's smile widened. "Because the Ash Court has plans for you, child of fire. And now that you've awakened the magic, it's time for you to take your place."

Valira's mind raced, Alyssia's words hanging in the air like smoke. Plans? The fire inside her flared in response, a warning. She took a step back, her eyes narrowing at the hunter before her.

"I'm not here to serve the Ash Court," Valira said, her voice steadier than she felt. "I came for answers, not to be used."

Alyssia's smile didn't waver. "Oh, I'm not asking you to serve. I'm offering you the chance to lead."

The words sent a shock through Valira, and she glanced at Caelan, whose expression had darkened. "Lead?"

"Yes," Alyssia replied, her gaze intense. "The Ash Court has waited for someone like you, someone who can unite fire and ice. Your mother's failure created fear, but you—you've succeeded. With that power, you could control the elements. You could rule the Ash Court."

Valira's heart pounded. Rule the Ash Court? The very idea seemed impossible, absurd. But Alyssia's eyes gleamed with conviction, as though she truly believed in what she was saying.

"I'm not here to rule," Valira said, her voice quieter now. "I don't want to be part of this war."

Alyssia stepped closer, her voice dropping to a near-whisper. "You don't have a choice, Valira. The courts will never let you walk away. You've touched the power now. You're a part of this, whether you like it or not."

Valira's hands trembled, the fire and ice swirling uneasily inside her. She could feel the truth in Alyssia's words. She had come here seeking answers, but in doing so, she had become something more. She had awakened a power that the courts would never allow to go unchecked.

"We need to leave," Caelan said, his voice hard as he stepped forward, placing himself between Valira and Alyssia. "Now."

Alyssia's smile faded, her eyes narrowing. "Leave if

you wish. But know this, Valira—if you walk away, the Ash Court will hunt you. They will see you as a threat, just as they saw your mother."

Valira's heart raced. She had known the risks, but hearing them spoken aloud made them feel all the more real. If she didn't accept Alyssia's offer, she would be running forever, caught between the courts and the power she couldn't fully control.

Caelan's hand was on her arm now, his touch grounding her. "We don't need her," he whispered. "We can find another way."

Valira met his gaze, her mind spinning. The fire inside her flared, the heat rising in her chest, but she forced it down, her breath shaky as she turned back to Alyssia.

"No," she said, her voice firm. "I won't be your weapon."

Alyssia's eyes flashed with anger, but she didn't move. "So be it. But don't say I didn't warn you."

———

With Alyssia's warning ringing in her ears, Valira and Caelan turned and walked out of the chamber, the heat of the Ash Court's magic still burning in her veins. Every step felt heavier than the last, the weight of what had just happened pressing down on her chest.

"We need to get out of here," Caelan said quietly as

they moved through the winding corridors of the court. "Before the others realize what you've done."

Valira nodded, though her mind was still whirling. Alyssia had offered her the chance to rule, to lead the Ash Court, but Valira had turned her back on that power. She didn't want it. She didn't want to be part of this war.

But as they reached the gates of the Ash Court, Valira couldn't shake the feeling that Alyssia had been right about one thing—there was no escaping the war. She had touched the power, and now it was part of her, a bond she couldn't break.

The fire and ice inside her were balanced, for now. But how long would that balance last? And what would happen when it tipped too far in one direction?

As they stepped out into the cold night air, Valira took a deep breath, her hands trembling as the reality of what lay ahead began to sink in.

They weren't running anymore. They were headed straight into the storm.

CHAPTER 6
STORM ON THE HORIZON

The cold night air bit at Valira's skin as she and Caelan moved swiftly through the outskirts of the Ash Court. The heat of the city still lingered in her veins, the fire and ice inside her balanced but tense, like two predators circling each other, waiting to strike. Every step they took away from the court felt like a small victory, but Valira couldn't shake the feeling that something was watching them.

Caelan's hand remained firmly on the hilt of his sword as he scanned the path ahead, his expression grim. "We need to move faster," he muttered, his eyes flicking back toward the city. "They won't let us get far."

Valira's heart raced, her pulse quickening with every glance back at the towering gates behind them. She could feel the magic of the Ash Court pressing against her, like a tether that threatened to pull her back. She had rejected Alyssia's offer, but that didn't mean the court would let her go.

"They're going to come for us, aren't they?" Valira asked quietly, her voice tight with fear.

Caelan didn't meet her gaze, but his silence was answer enough. He had known the risks when they entered the Ash Court. Now, they were on borrowed time.

"They'll send hunters," he said at last, his tone grim. "But we can lose them if we keep moving."

Valira swallowed hard, her breath fogging in the cold air. She had expected this, had known the moment she walked away from Alyssia that she would be branded a traitor to the court. But the reality of being hunted—of being pursued for the power inside her— was far more terrifying than she had imagined.

They moved quickly, slipping into the shadows of the dense forest that surrounded the Ash Court. The ground beneath them was hard, cracked with ash from years of fire, but as they pushed deeper into the woods, the earth softened, giving way to the frost and snow of the borderlands.

"We'll rest once we're clear of the Ash Court's terri-tory," Caelan said, his voice low as he glanced back again. "For now, we need to stay ahead of them."

Valira nodded, though her body was already aching from the long journey. She could feel the tension in

Caelan, the urgency in his every movement. He was right. They couldn't afford to stop. Not yet.

As they wove through the trees, Valira's thoughts turned to the fire and ice inside her. The magic she had awakened in the Ash Court was powerful—more powerful than anything she had felt before. But it had left her shaken, her mind spinning with doubts. What if she lost control again? What if the balance between the two elements slipped?

"We'll find a way to stop this," Caelan said, his voice softer now as if sensing her unease. "We'll find a way to end the war."

Valira looked up at him, her heart tightening in her chest. He spoke with such certainty, such quiet determination, but the path ahead felt anything but clear.

"How?" she asked, her voice barely above a whisper. "The courts are at war, and both want me for my powers. How can we stop them when I don't even understand what I've become?"

Caelan paused, his gaze softening as he turned to face her. "We'll figure it out together."

His words were a small comfort, but Valira knew there were no easy answers. The fire and ice inside her were part of something much larger—a war that had been raging for generations. And now, she was caught in the center of it.

They pushed forward through the forest, the trees growing thicker as they moved deeper into the borderlands. But just as they reached the edge of a clearing, Caelan stopped suddenly, his hand shooting out to grab Valira's arm.

"Wait," he whispered, his eyes narrowing as he scanned the shadows ahead. "Do you hear that?"

Valira's heart pounded in her chest as she strained her ears, listening for any sign of movement. For a long moment, there was nothing but the sound of the wind rustling through the trees. But then, faintly, she heard it —a low, distant hum, like the crackling of fire.

"They're coming," Caelan said, his voice tight. "We need to move. Now."

The crackle of fire grew louder behind them, and Valira's heart raced as she and Caelan sprinted through the trees. The air felt heavier, thicker with heat, as if the Ash Court's hunters had brought the flames with them. Valira's breath came in short gasps, her legs burning from the effort, but she didn't dare slow down.

"They're too close," Caelan muttered under his breath, his hand still on the hilt of his sword. "We need to lose them."

Valira's mind raced. She had felt the presence of the hunters long before they arrived—the magic they carried was like a beacon, pulling at her fire, trying to draw it out. But she couldn't let them catch her. She couldn't let them take her back.

"Up ahead," Caelan said, his voice low as he motioned toward a dense thicket of trees. "We can lose them in there."

They veered off the path, slipping through the thick underbrush, their footsteps muffled by the snow-covered ground. The trees here were taller, their branches casting long shadows over the forest floor. Valira's pulse quickened as they moved deeper into the thicket, the sounds of pursuit fading slightly behind them.

But just as she thought they might have escaped, a blast of heat exploded to their left, sending a wall of flames roaring through the trees.

Valira cried out, stumbling back as the fire surged toward them, the heat searing her skin. She could feel the fire inside her reacting, rising to meet the flames, but she fought to keep it under control.

Caelan grabbed her arm, pulling her to the side as another burst of fire erupted from the trees. "This way!" he shouted, leading her toward a narrow path that wound deeper into the woods.

They sprinted down the path, the fire still crackling behind them, but the trees were thick here, and the flames struggled to follow. Valira's heart pounded in her chest, her mind racing with fear and adrenaline. They couldn't keep running forever.

"We can't outrun them," Valira gasped, her breath coming in ragged gasps. "What do we do?"

Caelan's jaw clenched as he glanced back at the wall of fire creeping toward them. "We'll have to fight."

Valira's stomach twisted with fear. She had fought before—she had unleashed her powers in moments of desperation—but this was different. This wasn't about survival. This was about facing the full force of the Ash Court's hunters.

"We'll make a stand here," Caelan said, his voice steady as he drew his sword. "Use the trees for cover. We can't let them corner us."

Valira nodded, though her hands trembled with fear. She could feel the fire rising inside her, the heat building in response to the threat. But the ice remained still, buried beneath the flames.

They took cover behind a cluster of trees, the fire crackling in the distance. Valira's heart raced as she waited, her breath coming in short, shallow gasps. She could feel the hunters closing in, their magic pressing against her, pulling at the fire inside her.

"We'll be ready," Caelan whispered, his eyes locked on the path ahead.

Valira swallowed hard, her hands trembling as she reached for her powers. She couldn't lose control—not now. Not when everything depended on it.

The fire inside her flared, the heat rising in her

chest, but she forced herself to focus. She needed the ice. She needed the balance.

But as the hunters drew closer, their magic crackling in the air, Valira felt the fire slipping from her control. The flames roared to life inside her, burning hotter than ever before, and the ice remained locked away, unreachable.

She wasn't ready for this. Not yet.

The first of the hunters appeared through the trees, their cloaks flickering with fire as they moved toward them. Valira's pulse quickened, her breath coming in ragged gasps as the fire inside her surged, desperate to be unleashed.

Caelan raised his sword, his stance steady as the hunters closed in. "Stay behind me," he said, his voice firm. "I'll hold them off."

Valira shook her head, her heart racing. "I can't let you fight them alone."

"You don't have a choice," Caelan muttered, his gaze fixed on the approaching hunters. "If you use your powers now, they'll know exactly where you are."

Valira's hands trembled as she fought to keep the fire in check. She knew he was right. The moment she unleashed her powers, the hunters would sense it. But how could they fight without it?

The first hunter raised their hand, and a wall of fire erupted from their palm, surging toward them. Caelan moved quickly, stepping in front of Valira and deflecting the flames with a burst of icy magic. The air hissed as the fire collided with ice, steam rising in a thick cloud.

Valira's heart pounded as she watched the battle unfold. Caelan was skilled, his movements precise as he parried the hunters' attacks, but the fire was relentless, and the heat only grew stronger.

"We need to move!" Caelan shouted, his voice barely audible over the roar of the flames.

Valira nodded, but her body felt frozen, her legs heavy with fear. The fire inside her was too strong. It wanted to burn. It wanted to be free.

But if she let it out now, she knew it would consume everything.

As the next blast of fire surged toward them, Caelan deflected it again, but his movements were slower now, his strength waning. The hunters pressed forward, their magic crackling in the air, and Valira could feel the flames closing in.

"We don't have a choice," Caelan muttered, his voice filled with frustration. "We have to run."

Valira swallowed hard, her mind racing. They couldn't keep running forever. The Ash Court wouldn't stop hunting her. She had to find a way to fight back—to control the power inside her before it consumed them both.

But how?

———

Valira's hands shook as she struggled to keep the fire in check, her heart pounding as the heat inside her rose to a fever pitch. She could feel the flames clawing at her, desperate to be unleashed, but she couldn't—she couldn't let it take over.

The hunters moved closer, their magic pressing against her like a suffocating force. She could feel it pulling at the fire inside her, urging it to break free.

"Valira!" Caelan shouted, his voice filled with urgency as he deflected another blast of fire. "We have to move!"

Valira's pulse quickened, but her body felt frozen. The fire roared inside her, growing stronger with every moment, and she knew she couldn't hold it back much longer.

Suddenly, the ground beneath them trembled, and a blast of heat erupted from the earth, sending a shock-wave through the forest. Valira stumbled back, her breath catching in her throat as the fire inside her surged, pushing against her control.

The hunters stopped, their eyes fixed on her, and Valira knew in that moment that they had sensed it— the power inside her. They knew who she was.

And now, they were coming for her.

Caelan's eyes widened in alarm as he saw the change in the hunters. "Valira, no—don't!"

But it was too late.

The fire broke free.

The flames erupted from Valira's hands in a violent surge, crashing against the trees and igniting everything in their path. The forest lit up with a brilliant blaze, the heat roaring as the fire spread, wild and uncontrollable.

Valira's heart pounded as the fire consumed everything, her body trembling with the sheer force of the power she had unleashed. The hunters stumbled back their faces filled with shock as the flames surged toward them.

Caelan grabbed her arm, his eyes wide with fear. "Valira, stop! You have to stop!"

But she couldn't. The fire was too strong, too wild. It burned through her, untamable, and the ice inside her was nowhere to be found.

The forest burned, the trees crackling with flame as the fire roared to life. Valira gasped for breath, her chest tight with panic. She had lost control.

Again.

"I can't stop it," she cried, her voice barely audible over the roar of the flames. "It's too strong!"

Caelan's grip tightened on her arm, his voice urgent. "You have to try! You can't let it consume you!"

Valira squeezed her eyes shut, her heart racing as she fought to rein in the fire, but it was no use. The flames burned too hot, too fast, and the ice inside her was gone, lost in the heat.

"I can't," she gasped, her breath coming in ragged gasps.

Caelan pulled her closer, his voice low and desperate. "Yes, you can. You've done it before. You just need to find the balance."

Valira's hands trembled as she struggled to focus, her mind racing with fear and doubt. She could feel the fire burning inside her, but there was no ice to balance it. There was nothing but heat and flame.

But then, through the haze of fire and smoke, she felt it—a faint, flickering cold deep within her chest. It was weak, barely there, but it was enough.

She latched onto it, pulling it forward with everything she had.

Slowly, the fire began to subside, the flames flickering and dimming as the cold spread through her veins. The balance returned, fragile but present, and the fire finally died out.

Valira collapsed to the ground, her body trembling with exhaustion. The forest was scorched, the trees blackened and charred, but the fire was gone.

Caelan knelt beside her, his face etched with worry. "Are you okay?"

Valira nodded weakly, her breath coming in shallow gasps. "I... I think so."

But as she took in the devastation, her heart sank. She had lost control again. And this time, the damage was worse than ever.

The hunters had fled, but Valira knew they would be back. And next time, she might not be so lucky.

"We can't stay here," Caelan said quietly, his voice filled with urgency. "We need to keep moving."

Valira nodded, though her body ached with exhaustion. The fire and ice were still inside her, but the balance felt more fragile than ever.

They were running out of time.

CHAPTER 7

THE PRICE OF POWER

The cold wind howled through the trees as Valira and Caelan moved deeper into the frozen wilderness, leaving the charred remains of the forest behind them. The air felt heavier, thick with the weight of what had just happened. Valira's body still trembled with the aftershocks of the power she had unleashed. The balance of fire and ice inside her had become more fragile, slipping through her grasp with every step she took.

Caelan kept a steady pace beside her, his expression grim but focused. He hadn't spoken much since they fled from the hunters, but Valira could feel the tension radiating from him. They had barely escaped the Ash Court's grasp, and Valira had almost lost control of her powers again—only this time, the damage had been far worse.

"I'm sorry," Valira whispered, her throat tight with guilt. She hadn't meant for things to get so out of hand, but the fire inside her had become too strong, too wild.

Caelan glanced at her, his jaw tight. "You don't have to apologize."

Valira's heart sank. "Yes, I do. I put both of us in danger. If you hadn't been there…"

Caelan shook his head, his voice firm. "You can't control what's inside you, not yet. But you will. I'm not leaving you to face this alone."

His words, though meant to comfort, felt heavy. Valira wanted to believe him, wanted to believe that one day she could truly balance the fire and ice without losing herself. But after what had just happened, doubt gnawed at her. How many more times would she lose control? How much more destruction would follow in her wake?

The fire inside her still simmered, waiting for the next chance to erupt, while the ice remained faint, a distant presence she could barely touch. And now, with the Ash Court hunting her and the threat of war looming over both kingdoms, the stakes had never been higher.

They walked in silence for what felt like hours, the sky darkening as the sun began to set behind the mountains. The cold was growing sharper, biting at Valira's skin, but she barely noticed. Her thoughts were consumed with the memories of the day, of the fire she had unleashed, of the hunters she had nearly destroyed.

As they neared the edge of a frozen river, Caelan finally spoke. "We need to find shelter for the night. We can't keep moving in this cold."

Valira nodded, her body aching with exhaustion. She hadn't realized how drained she was until now, her limbs heavy from the weight of the day's events. The forest had thinned, leaving them exposed to the elements, and the temperature had dropped significantly.

"There," Caelan said, pointing toward a rocky outcropping at the base of a hill. "We can make camp there."

They moved quickly, their footsteps crunching in the snow as they made their way to the shelter. The outcropping provided some protection from the wind, and Caelan set to work gathering wood for a fire.

Valira sat down, her breath visible in the cold air as she wrapped her cloak tightly around her shoulders. Her mind was still spinning, her heart heavy with uncertainty. She had come so far, and yet the road ahead felt even more uncertain than before.

"What do we do next?" she asked quietly, watching as Caelan lit the fire.

"We keep moving," Caelan replied, his voice steady. "We need to get farther from the Ash Court before they send more hunters."

Valira's stomach twisted at the thought. The Ash Court wasn't going to stop. They wanted her power, and they wouldn't rest until they had it.

But it wasn't just the Ash Court that worried her. The Snow Court had its own reasons for wanting her dead, and sooner or later, they would come for her, too.

She was caught between two forces, both determined to use her or destroy her, and all the while, the power inside her continued to grow, threatening to tear her apart.

The fire crackled softly, casting flickering shadows over the rocky outcropping where they had settled for the night. Valira sat close to the flames, the warmth chasing away the biting cold of the night air, but the tension inside her was far from eased. The heat from the fire made her uncomfortable, a constant reminder of the power simmering just beneath her skin.

Across from her, Caelan sat silently, sharpening his blade in rhythmic strokes, the faint sound of metal against stone filling the quiet between them. His face was etched with concentration, but Valira knew the same thoughts weighed on him as they did on her—what would happen next? How long could they run before the Ash Court caught up again?

"You've been quiet," Caelan said after a long stretch

of silence, not looking up from his work. His tone was neutral, but Valira could hear the concern laced within it.

Valira bit her lip, her eyes fixed on the flickering flames. "I've been thinking," she said softly. "About what Alyssia said. About the power... and the war."

Caelan finally looked up, his gaze steady but unreadable. "What about it?"

Valira hesitated, unsure how to put her thoughts into words. "What if she was right?" she asked, her voice barely more than a whisper. "What if this power is meant to be used? What if I'm supposed to... rule?"

Caelan's eyes darkened, and for a moment, he didn't respond. The silence stretched between them, heavy with tension.

"You're not like them, Valira," he said finally, his voice low but firm. "Alyssia wants to use you for her own gain. The Ash Court doesn't care about you. They care about what you can do."

Valira frowned, her chest tightening. "But what if I could stop the war? What if I could use this power to end all of it?"

"And at what cost?" Caelan countered, his gaze hard. "The fire and ice inside you—those powers have torn kingdoms apart. Your mother tried to unite them, and it destroyed her. You saw what happened today when you lost control. Do you really think you can wield that kind of power without consequences?"

Valira's heart ached at his words, the truth of them sinking deep into her bones. He was right. She had seen firsthand how dangerous her powers were. Every time she used them, she risked losing herself, losing control. But the idea of sitting back, of running while the courts fought over her, felt unbearable.

"I don't want to run forever," she said quietly, her voice trembling. "I don't want to be hunted like some weapon."

Caelan's expression softened, and he set his sword aside, leaning forward slightly. "I know. But we're not running forever. We're looking for answers, for a way to control this. That's different."

Valira shook her head, the frustration building inside her. "But what if there isn't a way? What if I'm just delaying the inevitable?"

Caelan's gaze didn't waver. "Then we'll face that when it comes. But we're not giving up. Not yet."

Valira's breath caught in her throat as she met his gaze. He had stood by her this whole time, even when she had nearly destroyed everything with her powers. He hadn't left her, hadn't let her fall. And now, as the war loomed over them, he was still here, still willing to fight for her.

"Thank you," she whispered.

Caelan nodded once, his eyes still locked on hers. "We're in this together, Valira. We'll figure it out. But right now, you need to rest."

Valira nodded, though the fire and ice inside her felt far from calm. She knew sleep wouldn't come easily, not with the weight of what lay ahead pressing down on her.

As the night deepened and the fire burned low, Valira settled back, her mind still spinning with thoughts of the future. She had the power to change everything, but what would she sacrifice in exchange?

———

The pale light of dawn crept through the trees as Valira stirred from a fitful sleep. The fire had long since burned down to embers, leaving only the faint warmth of the ashes behind. Caelan was already awake, standing at the edge of their makeshift camp, his eyes scanning the horizon for any sign of movement.

Valira sat up, rubbing the sleep from her eyes. Her body ached with exhaustion, but her mind was sharper than it had been the night before. The fear that had gripped her so tightly seemed to have eased, replaced by a flicker of something else—hope.

"We should keep moving," Caelan said quietly, glancing over at her. "The farther we get from the Ash Court, the better."

Valira nodded, clasping the front of her cloak as she stood. The cold air bit at her skin, but she welcomed it, using the chill to steady the fire still simmering inside her. She could feel the balance slipping again, but for now, she had control.

As they packed up their camp and prepared to head deeper into the wilderness, Valira's thoughts drifted back to the conversation they'd had the night before. Caelan had been right—there was no easy answer, no clear path forward. But that didn't mean she was powerless.

"I've been thinking," Valira said as they started walking, her voice hesitant. "Maybe there's someone who can help us. Someone who knows more about... this."

Caelan glanced at her, his brow furrowed. "Who?"

Valira bit her lip, uncertain if she should say it. "My mother's old advisor. I don't know if he's still alive, but he might know more about her experiments. About how she tried to unite the courts."

Caelan's eyes darkened. "You think he'd be willing to help?"

Valira shrugged, though her heart was racing. "I don't know. But it's worth a try, isn't it?"

Caelan was quiet for a moment, his gaze thoughtful. "It's a risk. If he's still loyal to the courts, he could betray us."

"I know," Valira said softly. "But we're running out of options. If we don't figure this out soon, the courts will catch up to us, and we'll be right back where we started."

Caelan nodded slowly, his expression grim. "Then we find him."

Valira's heart leapt with a mix of fear and excitement. This could be their chance to get some answers, to understand what her mother had been trying to do. But it was also a gamble, one that could lead them straight into the hands of their enemies.

As they continued through the forest, the path ahead felt more uncertain than ever, but for the first time in days, Valira felt there was a way forward, and she wasn't facing it alone.

———

The sun had risen higher by the time they reached the outskirts of the small village nestled at the edge of the forest. The air was still cold, but the village was alive with activity—smoke rising from chimneys, people moving about with purpose. It was a quiet, isolated place, far from the reach of the courts, and for a moment, Valira felt a sense of relief.

"This is where he lives?" Caelan asked, his voice low as they approached the village.

Valira nodded. "At least, this is where he lived the last time I heard about him. It's been years, but if anyone knows about my mother's experiments, it's him."

Caelan's hand hovered near his sword, his eyes scanning the village with caution. "Let's hope he's still on our side."

They made their way through the village, keeping to the shadows as they approached a small, weathered cottage at the edge of town. Valira's heart pounded in her chest as they neared the door. She hadn't seen her mother's advisor since she was a child, but the memories of him were clear—a man of wisdom, but also of secrets. If anyone could help her understand the power inside her, it was him.

Valira hesitated at the door, her hand hovering over the handle. Caelan stood beside her, his expression tense.

"You don't have to do this alone," he said quietly.

Valira nodded, taking a deep breath before knocking.

For a long moment, there was silence. Then, slowly, the door creaked open, revealing a tall, thin man with graying hair and intelligent eyes. He looked at Valira, his gaze narrowing as if trying to place her.

"You," he said at last, his voice rough. "I never thought I'd see you again."

Valira swallowed hard. "We need your help."

The man's eyes flicked to Caelan, then back to Valira. "I'm not sure I can offer the kind of help you're looking for."

Valira stepped forward, her heart racing. "You knew my mother. You knew what she was trying to do. Please, I need to understand what's happening to me."

The man's expression softened slightly, but there was still wariness in his gaze. "I can tell you some things. But be warned, child—there are some secrets that are better left buried."

———

Valira and Caelan stepped inside the small, dimly lit cottage, the smell of old books and herbs filling the air. The man, whose name was Alaric, motioned for them to sit at a worn wooden table. His eyes lingered on Valira, as though seeing her brought back memories he'd long tried to forget.

"You want to know about your mother," Alaric said, his voice low as he settled into a chair across from them. "You want to know about the power she tried to wield."

Valira nodded, her hands trembling slightly. "Yes. I need to understand what she was trying to do. And... how to control it."

Alaric's expression darkened, and he leaned back in his chair, folding his hands in his lap. "Your mother was a brilliant woman, but she was also reckless. She believed she could unite fire and ice, bring balance to the two elements. But what she didn't understand was the cost."

Valira's heart raced. "What cost?"

Alaric's gaze shifted to the small fire burning in the hearth, the flames casting flickering shadows over his face. "The magic your mother was playing with—it wasn't natural. Fire and ice are opposing forces, always in conflict. She thought she could control them, bind them together, but in the end, they consumed her."

Valira's stomach twisted. She had known her mother's experiments had gone wrong, but hearing it spoken aloud made the reality of it all sink in.

"Is there a way to control it?" Valira asked, her voice trembling. "Is there a way to stop it from... consuming me?"

Alaric's eyes met hers, and for a moment, there was only silence.

"There might be," he said finally, his voice heavy with warning. "But it will come at a price. One that you might not be willing to pay."

Valira's breath caught in her throat. "What do you mean?"

Alaric's expression grew darker still. "The balance you seek—the power you wish to control—it requires a sacrifice. Your mother was willing to make that sacrifice, but in the end, she couldn't."

Valira's heart pounded in her chest. "What kind of sacrifice?"

Alaric's gaze hardened. "The kind that changes you forever."

The room seemed to close in around her, the weight

of Alaric's words pressing down on her chest. Valira had come here seeking answers, but the truth was more terrifying than she had imagined.

Caelan leaned forward, his voice low. "What kind of sacrifice are we talking about?"

Alaric's eyes flicked to Caelan his expression unreadable. "You'll find out soon enough."

CHAPTER 8

THE SACRIFICE OF POWER

T he air in Alaric's cottage felt thick, heavy with secrets long kept and whispered warnings. Valira sat at the worn table, her heart pounding in her chest as Alaric's words echoed in her mind: It requires a sacrifice. Your mother couldn't make it, but you must if you want control.

Caelan sat beside her, his hand resting on his sword, his expression tense. He hadn't spoken since Alaric's revelation, but Valira could feel the weight of his gaze, the unspoken question hanging between them. Was she willing to pay the price?

Valira swallowed hard, her throat dry. "What kind of sacrifice?" she asked again, her voice barely above a whisper.

Alaric leaned back in his chair, his sharp eyes studying her carefully. "Your mother believed she could unite the elements of fire and ice, bind them together in perfect harmony. She thought that by controlling both, she could end the conflict between the courts. But the balance between those forces is unnatural. They are meant to oppose each other."

Valira's hands trembled in her lap. She had felt that opposition, felt the fire and ice warring within her, constantly trying to tear her apart. But she had also felt brief moments of balance. Moments when the two forces had coexisted, however fragile that balance had been.

"So, it's impossible?" Caelan asked, his tone sharp. "No one can control both?"

Alaric's expression darkened. "Not without great cost. To bind those elements together, to maintain balance, you must give up something in return. Something that will allow you to become the vessel for that power."

Valira's heart raced, fear creeping into her chest. "What would I have to give up?"

Alaric hesitated, his gaze flicking between Valira and Caelan before he spoke. "Your humanity."

The words hit Valira like a blow, and she felt the air leave her lungs. Her mind raced, trying to grasp what Alaric was saying.

"My humanity?" she repeated, her voice shaking.

Alaric nodded, his expression grim. "The fire and ice inside you—they are forces beyond the mortal realm. To control them fully, to unite them, you must surrender part of yourself to the elements. You will become a conduit for the magic, but in doing so, you will lose something essential to who you are."

Valira's stomach twisted. "What did my mother lose?"

Alaric's gaze softened, a flicker of sadness in his eyes. "She never completed the ritual. She couldn't bear the thought of what it would do to her. She feared it would make her something... other. Something inhuman."

Valira's pulse quickened, her thoughts racing. Could she do what her mother hadn't? Could she give up part of herself to control the power that burned within her? The idea terrified her, but the alternative—losing control completely, being hunted by both courts—was equally horrifying.

"There's no other way?" Caelan asked, his voice low and tense.

Alaric shook his head. "If you want true control, there's no other way."

Valira stared at the table, her heart hammering in her chest. She had come here seeking answers, but now she wasn't sure if she wanted them.

"You don't have to decide now," Alaric said quietly. "But the longer you wait, the more dangerous the magic inside you becomes."

Valira nodded numbly, the weight of the decision

pressing down on her. She had always known her powers came with a price, but she hadn't realized how high that price would be.

The sun was setting by the time Valira and Caelan left Alaric's cottage, the sky painted in hues of orange and purple as the light faded behind the mountains. The village was quiet, the cold air nipping at Valira's skin as they walked through the narrow streets, but her mind was far from the present.

Give up part of yourself. Lose your humanity.

The words echoed in her mind, over and over, as if they had taken root inside her. She couldn't stop thinking about what that meant—what it would mean for her if she went through with the ritual. She had spent so much of her life trying to understand the fire and ice within her, trying to balance them. But to give up part of herself to control them? That wasn't something she had ever imagined.

"You're quiet," Caelan said, his voice breaking through her thoughts.

Valira looked up, meeting his gaze. His expression was tense, worried, but there was something else there, too—something that looked like fear.

"I'm just... thinking," Valira said softly, her breath fogging in the cold air.

Caelan slowed his pace, turning to face her fully. "You don't have to do this," he said firmly. "There has to be another way."

Valira bit her lip, her heart aching. She wanted to believe him, wanted to believe that there was another way to control the power without sacrificing a part of herself. But Alaric's words had been clear. The fire and ice weren't meant to coexist. To control them, she had to give up something in return.

"What if there isn't?" Valira asked quietly, her voice trembling. "What if this is the only way?"

Caelan's jaw clenched, and he shook his head. "I don't accept that. You've been fighting for control this whole time, and you've made it this far. You don't have to give up who you are to win."

Valira's chest tightened, her emotions swirling inside her. "But what if I lose control again? What if next time, the fire doesn't stop?"

"You won't," Caelan said, his voice fierce. "I won't let that happen."

Valira's breath caught in her throat, and for a moment, she couldn't speak. She wanted to believe him, wanted to trust that he could protect her from herself. But deep down, she knew that the decision was hers alone.

"I need time to think," she said finally, her voice barely above a whisper. "I need to figure out what I'm willing to give up."

Caelan's expression softened, and he nodded slowly. "We'll figure it out. Together."

Valira forced a small smile, though her heart felt heavy with the weight of the choice before her. She didn't know if she could make that sacrifice—didn't know if she was strong enough to lose part of herself for the sake of power.

That night, they camped on the outskirts of the village, the fire crackling softly as Valira sat beside it, staring into the flames. The warmth of the fire was a sharp contrast to the cold night air, but the heat made her uneasy, reminding her of the power she carried within her.

Caelan sat a short distance away, keeping watch as the darkness deepened. He had been quiet since their conversation earlier, but Valira could sense his worry, could feel the tension in the air between them.

Valira couldn't sleep. The weight of the decision she had to make pressed down on her, leaving her restless and anxious. Every time she closed her eyes, she saw flashes of fire and ice, battling for control inside her. She saw her mother, standing at the edge of the abyss, unable to make the choice that would have given her control. And then she saw herself, standing in her mother's place, facing the same impossible choice.

She stood up quietly, careful not to wake Caelan, and walked a short distance from the camp. The cold air stung her skin, but she welcomed it, using the chill to calm the fire that still simmered inside her.

As she stood there, staring out at the distant mountains, she heard a faint rustling behind her. She turned sharply, her heart racing, but there was no one there. The forest was quiet, the only sound the soft rustle of the wind through the trees.

But something didn't feel right.

Valira took a step back, her instincts screaming that something was wrong. She glanced back toward the camp, but Caelan hadn't moved. He was still sitting by the fire, unaware of the danger lurking in the shadows.

Before she could react, a figure emerged from the trees, moving quickly toward her. Valira's heart leapt into her throat as she recognized the fiery red hair and sharp eyes of Alyssia, the hunter from the Ash Court.

"You didn't think I'd let you go that easily, did you?" Alyssia's voice was low, dangerous, as she stepped closer, the air around her crackling with heat.

Valira's pulse quickened, and she instinctively reached for the fire inside her, but Alyssia raised a hand, and a wall of flame erupted between them.

"Don't even try," Alyssia said, her voice cold. "You're coming with me, whether you like it or not."

Valira's heart raced as she faced Alyssia, the heat from the wall of flame pressing against her skin. She could feel the fire inside her rising, desperate to break free, but she knew Alyssia was stronger. The hunter had been trained to control the flames, and Valira had only just begun to understand her own power.

"I'm not going back," Valira said, her voice trembling but resolute. "I'm not your weapon."

Alyssia's lips curled into a cold smile. "You don't have a choice, child of fire. The Ash Court wants you. And they will have you."

Valira took a step back, her mind racing. She couldn't let Alyssia take her, couldn't let herself be used as a pawn in the war between the courts. But how could she fight someone so powerful?

Before she could think of a plan, Alyssia moved, her hand shooting out to send a blast of fire toward Valira. Valira barely had time to react, throwing up her own hands to block the attack. The fire collided with her power, and for a moment, the two forces were locked in a deadly struggle, the heat between them almost unbearable.

"You've gotten stronger," Alyssia said, her eyes gleaming with interest. "But you're still no match for me."

Valira gritted her teeth, her arms trembling as she fought to hold back the flames. The fire inside her roared in response, threatening to break free, but she forced it down, trying to maintain control. She couldn't lose herself to the fire, not now.

Alyssia pressed forward, her attacks relentless as she pushed Valira back, the flames growing hotter and more intense with every strike. Valira's breath came in short gasps, her body trembling with the effort of holding the fire at bay.

"I don't want to fight you," Valira gasped, her voice strained. "But I will if I have to."

Alyssia's smile widened. "Good. Then show me what you're made of."

With a sudden burst of energy, Valira let the fire surge forward, pushing Alyssia back with a wave of heat. The flames roared, crackling and sparking as the two forces collided. But even as Valira pushed her power to its limits, she knew it wouldn't be enough. Alyssia was too strong, too experienced.

And then, just as she felt herself losing control, Valira remembered the ice.

The fire had always been her weapon, but the ice was her balance. She could feel it, buried deep within her, waiting for her to call upon it. With a deep breath, Valira focused on the cold, pulling it forward even as the fire raged inside her.

The temperature dropped sharply, and Alyssia faltered for a moment, her eyes widening in surprise. Valira seized the opportunity, sending a blast of icy wind toward her, the cold cutting through the flames like a blade.

Alyssia stumbled back, her expression darkening. "You're full of surprises," she muttered, her voice filled with grudging respect.

But Valira didn't stop. She pressed forward, the ice swirling around her as the fire burned alongside it. For the first time, the two elements weren't fighting against each other—they were working together, balanced in a delicate dance of power.

"I told you," Valira said, her voice steady now. "I'm not your weapon."

Alyssia's eyes narrowed, and for a moment, Valira thought she would attack again. But the hunter hesitated, her gaze flicking to the fire and ice swirling around Valira. There was a glimmer of something in her expression—something that looked almost like fear.

"This isn't over," Alyssia said, her voice low and dangerous. "The Ash Court will come for you. And next time, you won't be able to run."

With that, she stepped back into the shadows, disappearing into the darkness as quickly as she had appeared. The wall of flame flickered and died, leaving only the faint scent of smoke in the air.

Valira stood frozen, her breath coming in ragged

gasps as the fire and ice inside her began to settle. She had done it. She had fought back—controlled the elements, even if only for a brief moment.

But the weight of Alyssia's warning hung heavy in the air. The Ash Court wasn't going to stop. They would come for her again, and next time, she might not be so lucky.

Caelan appeared at her side, his expression filled with concern. "Are you all right?"

Valira nodded, though her body still trembled with the aftershocks of the battle. "I think so."

Caelan's eyes darkened as he looked out into the darkness where Alyssia had vanished. "We need to move. If she's here, more hunters won't be far behind."

Valira nodded again, exhaustion settling over her like a heavy blanket. She had won this battle, but the war was far from over. The fire and ice inside her were still unstable, and the price of controlling them loomed over her.

As they packed up their camp and prepared to leave, Valira couldn't shake the feeling that the real danger was still ahead. The Ash Court wanted her, and the Snow Court wanted her dead. And in the end, the only way to survive might be to make the sacrifice she feared most.

CHAPTER 9

THE FINAL RECKONING

The wind howled through the mountains, sharp and biting as it whipped around Valira and Caelan. They had been traveling for hours, the landscape growing harsher with every step. The path ahead was steep and treacherous, but Valira hardly noticed the cold anymore. The fire and ice within her had reached a fragile equilibrium, and she could feel them both simmering under her skin, balanced for now but always threatening to spiral out of control.

Caelan walked a few paces ahead, his shoulders tense, his hand resting on the hilt of his sword. He had been silent since they had left the village, the weight of what lay ahead pressing down on both of them. They had escaped the Ash Court's hunters for now, but the threat still lingered, growing closer with every step they took.

"The pass is just ahead," Caelan said, his voice barely audible over the wind. "We'll be in neutral territory once we cross it."

Neutral territory. The space between the warring courts of Snow and Ash, a desolate stretch of land that neither kingdom controlled. It would offer them some protection, at least for a little while. But Valira knew it wouldn't last. The Ash Court was relentless, and the Snow Court wouldn't be far behind. They had only delayed the inevitable.

Valira's heart pounded as she followed Caelan up the rocky incline, her mind spinning with doubts. Every step they took brought them closer to a confrontation she wasn't ready for. Alyssia's words still echoed in her mind: The Ash Court will come for you. And next time, you won't be able to run.

"Do you think they'll follow us into neutral territory?" Valira asked, her voice tight with fear.

Caelan glanced back at her, his expression grim. "They won't stop. Not until they have what they want."

Valira swallowed hard. What they wanted—what the Ash Court wanted—was her. They wanted the power inside her, the fire and ice that could unite the courts or tear them apart. And they would stop at nothing to claim it.

She glanced at Caelan, her chest tightening. He had been with her through all of this, risking his life to protect her, to help her control the magic that threatened to consume her. But how long could they keep running? How long before they had to face the inevitable?

"We can't keep running forever," Valira said quietly, her voice trembling. "We'll have to fight them, eventually."

Caelan's jaw tightened, and for a moment, he didn't respond. Then, slowly, he nodded. "I know. But not yet. We need time to figure out our next move."

Valira nodded, though her heart was heavy with the weight of the decision she knew they would soon have to make. The balance of power inside her was fragile, and the price for controlling it loomed ever closer. But deep down, she knew there was no avoiding the final reckoning.

———

By the time they reached the pass, the sky had darkened, heavy clouds rolling in from the west. The wind had picked up, and snow began to fall in soft, swirling flakes, covering the rocky landscape in a thin blanket of white. Valira shivered, pulling her cloak tighter around her shoulders as they made their way through the narrow mountain pass.

"This place is deserted," Caelan said, his eyes scanning the rocky cliffs on either side. "No one's crossed through here in months."

Valira's pulse quickened as they descended into the valley, the sense of isolation growing with every step. The neutral territory stretched out before them, vast and empty, with no sign of life. It was a place of desolation, caught between the fires of the Ash Court and the frozen lands of the Snow Court.

"We're safe here for now," Caelan said, though his voice held little comfort. "But we need to keep moving."

Valira nodded, her mind still racing. The neutral territory offered a temporary reprieve, but it wouldn't protect them forever. They needed a plan, a way to stop the war before it destroyed everything.

As they crossed into the valley, the snow grew thicker, the cold more biting. The landscape shifted, the rocky ground giving way to frost-covered earth. Valira could feel the power of the Snow Court in the air, the icy magic that had always felt distant and untouchable now pressing in on her.

"We're close to the Snow Court's border," Caelan said, his eyes narrowing. "We'll need to be careful from here."

Valira nodded, but her thoughts were elsewhere. The Snow Court had wanted her dead from the beginning, fearing the power she carried. But now, she wasn't so sure if they were the real enemy. The Ash Court had been relentless in their pursuit, but the Snow Court had its own reasons for wanting her out of the way.

She had spent so much time running from both

courts, but now, she wondered if there was another way. If she could find a way to control the magic inside her, to unite fire and ice, could she stop the war? Could she end the conflict that had torn the courts apart for generations?

But the cost of control—the price of binding those forces together—still hung over her like a shadow. Alaric's words echoed in her mind: To bind fire and ice, you must give up part of yourself.

Was she willing to make that sacrifice?

As they moved deeper into the valley, Valira's thoughts were interrupted by the sound of footsteps crunching in the snow. She froze, her heart leaping into her throat.

"Caelan," she whispered, her voice filled with dread.

Caelan's hand shot to his sword, his eyes scanning the valley. "Stay close."

The footsteps grew louder, and from the shadows of the snow-covered rocks, figures began to emerge. Valira's heart pounded as she recognized the blackened armor and ash-streaked cloaks of the Ash Court's hunters.

They had found them.

―――――

Valira's pulse quickened as the hunters moved closer, their eyes glowing with the fiery magic of the Ash

Court. She could feel the fire inside her responding to their presence, stirring in her chest like a beast waking from slumber. But she forced it down, knowing that if she unleashed it now, she would lose control.

Caelan stood in front of her, his sword drawn, his body tense. "Stay behind me," he muttered, his voice low and urgent. "We can't let them surround us."

Valira nodded, her heart racing as she gripped the edges of her cloak, trying to steady her breathing. The cold air burned in her lungs, and the snow swirled, but she barely noticed. All her focus was on the hunters, their faces hidden behind masks of ash and soot.

"Valira of the Ash and Snow," one of the hunters called out, his voice echoing through the valley. "You cannot run from your fate. Surrender now, and we will show mercy."

Valira's stomach twisted, fear clawing at her chest. The fire inside her flared, desperate to break free, but she fought to keep it under control. She couldn't give in to the fire. Not now.

Caelan stepped forward, his sword gleaming in the fading light. "She's not going anywhere with you."

The hunter's eyes narrowed and his voice filled with contempt. "You are nothing but a traitor to the Ash Court. You have no right to speak."

Caelan's jaw tightened, and Valira could see the tension in his stance. He was ready to fight, but there were too many of them. They were outnumbered.

"I won't go back with you," Valira said, her voice trembling but firm. "I'm not your weapon."

The hunter's eyes gleamed with amusement. "You are the key to ending this war. The Ash Court does not need you to be willing."

Valira's heart pounded in her chest, her mind racing. She had to do something, but the fire and ice inside her were warring, threatening to break loose at any moment. She needed to find the balance, but it felt so far out of reach.

Before she could react, the hunter raised his hand, and a wall of fire erupted from the ground, roaring toward them.

The heat of the flames rushed toward Valira and Caelan, but before they could be consumed, Caelan moved swiftly, raising his sword and sending a blast of icy magic toward the fire. The air hissed as the fire and ice collided, steam rising in a thick cloud between them.

"Go!" Caelan shouted, his voice filled with urgency. "Run while I hold them off!"

Valira's heart raced as she took a step back, but she couldn't leave him. Not again. She had lost control too many times before, had let Caelan fight her battles for her. But not this time. This time, she had to fight.

"No," Valira said, her voice steady despite the fear gnawing at her. "I'm not running."

She reached for the power inside her, the fire and ice that had always been in conflict. The flames burned hot in her chest, but the cold was there too, sharp and biting. She focused on the balance, on the delicate thread that connected the two forces, and for a brief moment, she felt it.

The fire and ice surged through her, not as enemies, but as equals. She raised her hands, and a blast of fiery ice erupted from her palms, crashing into the hunters with a force that sent them staggering back.

Caelan glanced at her in surprise, but he didn't question it. He turned back to the hunters, deflecting another blast of fire with his sword, while Valira pressed forward, her power swirling around her like a storm.

The hunters recovered quickly, their eyes blazing with fury as they moved in for the attack. But Valira didn't hesitate. She raised her hands again, the fire and ice inside her coiling together, and sent another wave of magic toward them, freezing the ground at their feet and sending flames crackling through the air.

The hunters faltered, their movements slowed by the ice, but they didn't stop. Valira could feel their magic pressing against hers, trying to break her control, but she held on, her body trembling with the effort.

"Valira, we need to move!" Caelan shouted, his voice filled with urgency.

Valira's heart raced as she took a step back, her power still crackling. The hunters were recovering, their magic burning hotter with every moment, and she knew they couldn't hold them off much longer.

With a final burst of energy, Valira sent a blast of fire and ice toward the hunters, buying them a few precious seconds. Then, without looking back, she turned and ran, Caelan close behind her.

They ran through the snow-covered valley, the sound of the hunters' pursuit fading behind them as they reached the edge of the pass. Valira's breath came in short, ragged gasps, her body trembling from the effort of controlling the magic inside her. She had fought back, had found the balance between fire and ice, but it had taken everything she had.

Caelan grabbed her arm, pulling her behind a cluster of rocks as they caught their breath. "Are you all right?"

Valira nodded, though her body ached with exhaustion. "I think so."

Caelan's eyes were filled with worry as he looked at her. "You found the balance."

Valira swallowed hard, her heart still racing. "For now. But it won't last."

Caelan's jaw tightened, but he didn't argue. He knew as well as she did that the balance was fragile, and the next time she lost control, the consequences could be catastrophic.

"We need to keep moving," Caelan said quietly. "The hunters will regroup soon."

Valira nodded, though her mind was spinning. The power inside her had always been a curse, something she had feared and fought against. But now, she was beginning to understand what Alaric had meant. The balance between fire and ice wasn't just about control—it was about sacrifice.

She had felt it in the battle, the way the magic had pulled at her, demanding more. If she wanted true control, if she wanted to stop the war, she would have to give in to that power. But what would it take from her?

As they moved through the valley, the snow falling softly, Valira knew the time for running was coming to an end. The Ash Court and the Snow Court were closing in, and soon, she would have to make a choice.

To end the war, she would have to embrace the magic inside her. But doing so would mean losing a part of herself forever.

And once she crossed that line, there would be no turning back.

The End.

Did you enjoy Valira and Caelan's story?
Please rate or review it on Amazon, Goodreads,
Bookbub, or your favorite retailer.

Read *A Curse of Thorns and Slumber*, the next book in the *Legends Reborn* series.

For updates, sales, and promotions, join my newsletter
at
mhlebeaultauthor.substack.com

ABOUT THE AUTHOR

Positive, uplifting books and stories.

Marie-Hélène Lebeault is the author of *The Evers Series, Clarity Castle, What Happens Next? Readers Decide Which Story Becomes a Book, the Blood Magick Trilogy, Holiday Shifters, Ghost Stories, Defenders of the Realm, Utopia, Chronicles of the Starborne Cadets*, as well as a series of picture books called Fairy Grandmother. She lives in Canada with her grown children.

www.mhlebeault.com

Follow on Social Media, she'd love to hear from you!

facebook.com/mhlebeaultauthor

x.com/mhlebeault

instagram.com/mhlebeault

amazon.com/author/mhlebeault

bookbub.com/authors/marie-helene-lebeault

goodreads.com/mhlebeault

linkedin.com/in/mhlebeault

tiktok.com/@mhlebeaultauthor

Also by the Author

Legends Reborn (Fairytale Retellings)

A Curse of Snow and Ash

A Curse of Thorns and Slumber

A Curse of Glass and Shadows

A Curse of Silver and Scars

A Curse of Storm and Stone

A Curse of Sand and Smoke

The Chronicles of the Starborne Cadets

Confluence of Destinies

Stars Beyond Realms

Shadows of Orion

Echoes of the Void

The Nebula's Heart

The Starborne Paradox

Defenders of the Realm

A Journey to Power

The Quest for the Emerald Rattleback

A Summer of Discovery

The Quest for the Sacred Tree

A Summer of Opposites

The Quest for the Phantom Feather

A Summer of Courage

The Quest for the Kraken's Ink

A Summer of Destiny

The Quest for the Cursed Mirrors

A Summer of Unity

Defenders of the Realm - Special Edition Hardcover Set

The Battle of the Blossoming Flame (FREE!)

The Evers Series

The Ancestors' Key

The Academy

The Time Walker

The World Jumper

5th Anniversary Edition Omnibus

The Traveler's Handbook

The Lost Key

Blood Magick Trilogy

The Blood Mage

Blood Magick

Blood Legacy

Extended Edition Omnibus

Standalones

Clarity Castle

What Happens Next?

Ghost Stories

Holiday Shifters

Echoes of Tomorrow

Utopia

Picture Books

Fairy Grandmother: Millie Goes to Antarctica

Fairy Grandmother: Millie Goes to the North Pole

Fairy Grandmother: Millie Goes to China

Fairy Grandmother: Millie Goes to Africa

(Also available in French, Spanish, German, and Italian)